THE KURCHATOV PENETRATION

A Novel

Timothy S. Jacobson

Published by

Visjonær Press
201 Main St., Suite 1001
La Crosse, WI 54601

Cover design by Stephanie Fraase

ISBN-13: 978-0-9849598-0-8
ISBN-10: 0984959807

For Jacquelyn, and in memory of Ruth, 1955-2009

ACKNOWLEDGMENTS

I would like to acknowledge the assistance of William Hoffman who critiqued the manuscript, Stephanie Fraase who helped me transform the digital book to physical form, and many others who provided advice, information and encouragement along the way.

THE KURCHATOV PENETRATION

CHAPTER ONE

Moscow, Russia
January

Pyotr Yakushkin pulled a large, antiquated cell phone from his lab jacket pocket, and popped off the back, exposing a hollow interior. He dumped the contents, washer-shaped pieces of lead wrapped in tissue paper, into his gloved hand and set the package on a small table. The gloves couldn't conceal the physicist's trembling. He unfolded the tissue paper and slid the pieces of lead to one side.

He opened a locker, nothing more than those used in high schools, and selected a plastic tube from the dozens stored there. A man who'd worked with nuclear materials for twenty-six years, Yakushkin poured 97-percent-enriched uranium washers onto the tissue paper as casually as one would pour cereal into a bowl. He dumped several others directly on the table, stuffed the lead rings into the tube as replacements, and topped it off with the few uranium pieces on the table.

Then he returned the tube to the locker, nestling it behind several unmolested cylinders. He wrapped the remaining rings of uranium in the tissue paper and stuffed them into the cavity in the gutted-out phone. As he locked Building 116, he averted his eyes from the camera above the door.

This would be the last time, he assured himself. He accomplished the first two thefts without raising suspicion, and they'd paid him six times his annual salary in a lump sum for his trouble. But he could never shake the feeling he'd be caught eventually.

Yakushkin walked on the ice-covered path and approached the secured exit of the Kurchatov Institute, headquarters of Russia's nuclear program. His heart raced as he entered the building where he'd have to be cleared before leaving the grounds.

The scientist had been a fixture at the institute for many years, and the guards greeted him with disinterest. Despite the exchange of pleasantries, Yakushkin couldn't stop thinking about the handguns the guards carried, and how easily they could shoot him.

He stepped onto the man trap, a device that weighed a person upon entering and again upon leaving, calculating any discrepancy as a warning of possible theft. The man trap would not betray him—he'd brought in precisely enough washers to offset the weight of the uranium.

He placed the phone and his keys in a tray as he stepped through the metal detector. A guard slid the tray along a table to the other side of the metal detector, then plucked the phone from the tray. Yakushkin froze in horror.

The young soldier studied the phone, examining it from several angles. He moved it up and down to feel its heft. "I'd be happy to have even an old cell phone like this, but I can't afford it if they don't pay me."

"It's handy, but I could use a smart phone," the scientist said, reaching for the phone but unable to grasp it.

"How does it work?" the guard asked, pressing the power button. Nothing happened, and he looked puzzled.

"Battery must be dead." Yakushkin put a hand on the table to allow himself to lean farther, and snatched the phone away. "I'll recharge it and show you sometime."

He walked past the elegant, bright yellow main building to his drab, brown car. He gazed at the huge bust of I.V. Kurchatov, father of the Soviet atom bomb, feeling a tinge of guilt. What would his scientific hero think of his life's work being plundered for personal wealth? he wondered. Then he noticed the shiny Mercedes parked nearby, and the guilt was replaced with contempt sparring with envy. Yakushkin knew the Mercedes had not been purchased from a regular salary.

The scientist drove a torturous route through a residential neighborhood for twenty minutes as he'd been instructed, nervously watching his rearview mirror to see if anyone followed. He stopped on a randomly chosen street, emptied the uranium from the phone, and stuffed the washers in the bottom of a white paper bag of pigeon food.

At a park along the Moskva River, he sat on a bench and fed a hungry flock. When the bag was half empty, he closed the top and rolled it tightly, placing it in the snow under the bench. He pulled an empty bag from his parka, opened it by inserting a fist, then carried the empty bag to his car as a decoy.

Two men in a silver BMW studied Yakushkin as he walked to his car with the empty bag. The driver rested his large head on his hand, elbow braced against the junction between the car door and window. The side of his face squished by his hand made his deep-set eyes sink lower. "It's about time the old coot stopped feeding those damned pigeons."

The passenger in the BMW looked barely eighteen, and he wondered how his partner could be so calm and act so bored with respect to their mission. The teenager fidgeted with a modified TEC-9 machine pistol in his lap, pulling the clip, examining the top round of ammunition, replacing the clip, and checking to ensure it was properly seated. "Yeah," he answered at last, "I want to get this over with."

"Nervous?" the driver asked, perking up with concern over whether his young companion would complete the task. "Don't worry, you'll have plenty of opportunities to practice 'taking out the garbage.'"

The young man pondered that statement for a moment, then asked, "What's the deal with this guy, anyway?"

The driver shrugged. "I don't know. I heard something about him refusing to cooperate anymore. What difference does it make? You'll get paid."

"I was just curious."

The BMW driver started the engine after Yakushkin passed by, and waited for the scientist to get a block and a half ahead before pulling out from the curb. They followed at a distance until Yakushkin turned down an empty side street.

Yakushkin drove toward home without bothering to look for a tail. He no longer possessed anything illegal, and he figured that if no one followed him to the park, no one would bother following him as he left.

The BMW roared as it closed the distance between the two vehicles. The young passenger lowered the window, and maintaining a tight grip on the TEC-9, repositioned his legs to suppress the shaking of his knees. Turning his head from the driver, he shut his eyes tightly for a moment and summoned from his gut the strength to carry out his assignment.

The silver car sped alongside the physicist's brown vehicle. The young man popped the TEC-9 up from his lap and braced himself on the door. The gun sputtered, and a shower of lead ripped through the car door and disintegrated the front windows. The bullets shredded Yakushkin's body, the interior of the car splattered with blood, pieces of lung and brain tissue, and fragments of bone.

The BMW skidded to a stop, allowing the scientist's car to coast onward into a parked car. The thugs spun around and raced from the scene.

Vienna, Austria

Vladimir Petrovich Stoletov sat at the desk in the corner of the grimy hotel room, running his fingers through his thinning hair, looking disgustedly at the carpeting blemished with numerous cigarette burns and larger stains. In the years since he left the old KGB, he'd grown accustomed to finer accommodations. Vienna had much better to offer, but he didn't come here on vacation. His companion, barrel-chested with a thick neck, sat on the bed inspecting a Tokarev pistol, unconcerned with his surroundings.

The knocks came, three quick ones followed by a pause before the fourth. Both men rose, the bulky one moving behind the door, his gun ready. Stoletov walked up to the door, taking comfort in the presence of his bodyguard and several more armed men in a room across the hall. "Who is it?" he asked in German.

"I'm from the photo shop. I have the pictures you dropped off."

The Russian opened the door. An Iranian, dressed like a tourist, entered. He carried a leather bag on a shoulder strap.

The stranger noticed the bodyguard and looked at the pistol. The bodyguard, seeing the man's hands in the open, holstered the gun inside his blazer.

"I'm Riza," the stranger said, extending his hand. The two Russians knew this was not his name, as he was a member of Etallat, the Iranian intelligence service.

Stoletov introduced himself as Viktor. He motioned toward one of two chairs on either side of a small table. They sat while the bodyguard locked the door.

In the custom of his Iranian guest, Stoletov made sure the table had been set with a teapot, small ceramic cups, a plate with filled with figs and dates, another with a stack of flatbread, and bowls of hummus and olives.

It would be rude for Stoletov to jump immediately into discussing business with an Iranian, and so the two discussed soccer and compared the weather in Russia and Iran while sampling the food and sipping mint tea.

After at least fifteen minutes of mundane conversation, Stoletov said, "I'm sorry to hear about the recent assassination of yet another nuclear scientist from Natanz," referring to a deputy director from the uranium enrichment facility in central Iran.

"The Mossad and CIA have been ruthless in targeting our nuclear experts and infrastructure. But we are persistent and determined. They will not stop us. You have it?" Riza asked.

"Yes, just over half a kilo—530 grams as we promised. You have the money?"

Riza nodded.

Stoletov picked up a camcorder from the table, popped open a side panel modified with a sheet of lead, and removed three thick plastic bags containing uranium washers.

Riza unzipped a fanny pack and, reaching slowly to avoid alarming his Russian business partners, extracted a pair of rubber gloves, a small file, a folding knife, tweezers, and a plastic vial filled with nitric acid. He donned the gloves, cut into one of the bags, and pulled out a washer from the middle of the stack. As he ran the file across the edge, a shower of sparks erupted, characteristic of uranium's rapid oxidation. With the tweezers, he picked up several small shavings and dropped them into the vial to test purity. He repeated this procedure with several washers from each bag. When finished with the test, he nodded, expressing his satisfaction.

Stoletov looked at Riza expectantly, and the Iranian handed the leather bag to him. The ex-KGB agent opened the satchel and peered inside. He removed a camcorder, a model identical to the one containing the uranium, and set it aside.

Then he pulled out about a dozen straps of euros, flipping the edges of the bills past his thumb to examine the money.

"You'll get the premium payment in one week after we've checked the quality of the entire batch," Riza said, returning the washers to the inside of the camcorder.

"There won't be a problem with quality," Stoletov assured him. "It's the best—space reactor fuel."

"It may be good, but it's still not nearly enough to reach critical mass. At this rate, it will take years to build a bomb, other than a mere radiation dispersal device. We'd be much better off with plutonium 239 than this *uranium*." Riza almost spat the last word. "Nikolai Volkov has been promising Fazullah larger quantities. If you can't supply it, we will turn elsewhere."

"Tell Fazullah he'll get plutonium 239 soon enough. We *will* provide critical mass."

CHAPTER TWO

Madison, Wisconsin
Early March

Two figures sat in the dark computer lab, their faces illuminated only by the glow of a single PC monitor. Two dozen more machines surrounded them, unknowing witnesses to the crime.

"Gene, this is the moment you've been waiting for," Kent said. "You've wanted to learn how to hack into a computer—now's your chance. Remember: you can't tell *anyone*, except anonymously on the Internet where you can brag to the whole world about your exploits."

"I'm not going to tell," Gene said.

Kent Dalton had dishwater-blond hair long and thin like his body. A precocious 17-year-old high school junior enrolled in two classes at the University of Wisconsin, Kent often assisted his father, John Dalton, an engineering professor, on research projects at the UW, particularly with software development for assorted medical-type analytical equipment.

John had long been involved in the design of analytical tools for the medical field and sometimes secured funding from the U.S. Department of Defense because of possible military applications for the technology he created. This funding permitted John, and Kent as well, to have access to some of the most expensive and advanced scientific equipment available.

Kent started taking college classes at the beginning of his junior year of high school. He could have completed high school in three years, but John thought it best his son stay with his peers even though he resented being held back.

Kent's interest in technology usually did not extend to the academic. He enjoyed the thrill of hacking into computer systems, and insatiable curiosity drove him to tinker with everything.

Gene, another high school junior, pudgy with brown hair, possessed many of the same interests as Kent but lacked his razor-sharp intellect and access to many of the educational opportunities Kent had. The town where Gene grew up had a population less than one-third the size of the enrollment in his current Madison high school. Eleven years earlier, his divorced mother remarried only to have her new husband lose his job. He found work in Madison a few years later, and Kent and Gene ended up in the same middle school.

"First of all," Kent said, "it often takes days of work to find vulnerabilities in a computer system. Often it's necessary to give up on a particular organization with good security and move on to another. Two things work in our favor. First, many system administrators aren't smart enough to find and fix their computers' weaknesses. Second, even if a sysadmin is smart, often he'll leave big holes in security for his own convenience.

"Any time you attack another system," Kent continued, "you need to use several layers of Internet accounts to prevent the authorities from tracing the attack back to you. I've got hacked accounts all over the place. You also need what's called a 'root kit' installed on the account at the end of the line. It will keep the ISP from knowing you're even using the system to carry out the attacks."

Kent logged into an unauthorized university computer account, used the telnet program to access a UNIX shell account at an ISP, from there reached another, and again to a fourth account.

"You want to see some cool shit?" Kent asked. "We're going to try some bank computers."

"Whoa. You sure you want to do banks?"

"They can't trace it back to us, and we're not going to steal anything. Don't worry. I've already found some computers we can try. I scanned their ports a week ago and found some possible entry points. We're going to try Internet Protocol spoofing. Let's start with First National Bank of Dane County."

Kent tried to connect through the Internet to a particular port on the First National machine. The response, a barrage of random alphanumeric characters, was instantaneous, filling the screen. The last computer in the series, through which the connection had been established, crashed.

"Damn!" Kent hit the table with his fist and shook his head in disgust. "They bombed us. Must have detected my scans last week and tightened security."

Kent reconnected to the last illicit account. "Screw that one for now. We'll try WisBanc. I've got a savings account, and my dad borrowed money for our house there."

Columns of numbers marched up the screen as the computer fired SYN packets at the bank's FTP server in the "DMZ area" outside the firewall, receiving ACK/SYN packets with sequence numbers in reply.

"We're not getting blown away by the daemon on this machine," Gene said, referring to an automatic utility program.

"Right," Kent agreed, "and fortunately they haven't done anything fancy with the initial sequence number."

"I don't understand quite how this IP spoofing works," Gene admitted.

"We'll pose as a friendly, or 'trusted,' computer on the organization's internal network. Normally, each computer on a network is identified by its Internet Protocol number, which is an 'address' affixed to each packet of data transmitted over the network. With internal networks, computers may grant unrestricted access to other computers by specifying their address numbers. We'll penetrate the security by impersonating the address of one of the specified internal computers, which I've already determined.

"The trick is," Kent continued, "once we know the initial sequence number and how much the sequence number is incremented with each packet, then we send a packet that pretends to be from one of the internal computers on their network. The server will respond with an acknowledge/synchronize packet to the internal computer we've impersonated, but that computer can't respond, because we'll tie it up with a denial of service attack. We don't receive the response that goes to the trusted computer, but since we know the next sequence number, we issue an ACK message with the predicted sequence number. Then we'll have established a connection in which we can send data. Let's try it.

Kent shot a SYN packet at the Rlogin port of the target server, and after a short delay, followed it with a packet with the ACK flag on.

"I think we're in," Kent said, smiling broadly.

"Now what do we do?" Gene asked, amazed.

"We're running blind, because the computer still thinks it's communicating with the internal machine. We have to insert a backdoor by modifying the '.rhosts' file. Then we can connect again without pretending to be another machine.

"If we wanted to brag on the Internet," Kent continued, "we'd have to come up with some credible evidence of our entry. In this case, we'll keep things quiet, so I can go back to the site later. We'll try to install a root kit, and cover our tracks."

Kent installed a backdoor by issuing a simple "echo '+ +' >> /.rhosts" command. Then he reconnected to the bank's computer. Within two hours, he'd managed to call up the balance of his savings account and his father's mortgage.

"Pretty cool, don't you think?" Kent asked.

"Yeah, but I'm uncomfortable digging around in a bank's files."

"What's the big deal? They've got a financial statement for my dad that tells them just about everything about *us*. All we're doing is looking at our own account information. I'm not prying in anyone else's bank balance. Besides, I'm doing the bank a favor. I'm going to close the hole so no one else can use IP spoofing on their system."

CHAPTER THREE

Moscow
Mid-March

Nikolai Mikhailovich Volkov stabbed his fist toward his cousin's face as if to hit the dime-size birthmark above his left eyebrow. Kirill Ivanovich Kardirov swung back with a glancing blow to Volkov's padded helmet. A smile could be seen on Volkov's sweaty face despite a mouth guard, expressing his thought that Kardirov's punch was good, but not good enough.

Volkov darted to the side to avoid the next jab. The leader of a powerful segment of the Russian *mafiya*, Volkov enjoyed sparring with his cousin in the boxing ring he occasionally rented for private use, with an armed guard standing watch at each exit. Volkov was a short man with thick, dark hair and broad, muscular shoulders. His surname means "wolf" in Russian, and he lived up to the name.

Kardirov oversaw most of the day-to-day business of his cousin's organization. Volkov trusted no one like he trusted Kardirov, and Kardirov worked hard to maintain that trust. He kept a close watch over the people working for them, as he had over his soldiers when he'd been a young army officer during the Soviet war in Afghanistan.

"Did Stoletov deliver the money from his trip to Vienna?" Volkov asked, punching at Kardirov.

"Yes, and he carried something else too—an ultimatum from Fazullah." Kardirov paused to suck in a breath before continuing. "We need to supply critical mass soon, or he'll take his business elsewhere. He's not happy with a little HEU. He wants several kilograms of P-239."

Volkov became angry with his inability to meet the Iranian's demand, angry at his subordinates and angry at himself. "Now that our dead Kurchatov physicist can't supply us with nuclear materials, we're going to have to find a way to supply ourselves."

Volkov unleashed his fury at his cousin, lunging with fists flying. He hit Kardirov squarely between the eyes, once then twice, jerking his head back. Gloves landed hard on Kardirov's midsection, then three more vicious blows to the head before he dropped to the floor. For an instant, Volkov imagined himself in one of his many childhood street fights, and he cocked his foot back, ready to kick Kardirov in the ribs.

Kardirov saw this, put his hands out as a shield, and looked up into Volkov's eyes. Volkov stopped himself and extended his hand to help Kardirov get up.

"I have some ideas for getting the plutonium Fazullah wants," Volkov said. "Tomorrow, we'll talk."

CHAPTER FOUR

Late April

Anatoly leaned back in his chair at the kitchen table reading *Nezavisimaya Gazeta*, trying to catch up on the news as he chewed a chunk of beef from thick, greasy soup he had prepared. A hint of early evening sunlight struggled past a blanket of gray clouds and through two west windows in his corner apartment. A pair of eyes with binoculars peered in his windows on the south side.

The lead story in the paper was nothing new—just more dismal economic information. The value of the ruble had plummeted further, the International Monetary Fund refused to extend more credit to Russia, and the government would be another month behind in wage payments to its employees.

Anatoly read with little concern for himself. He had less to fear from the financial catastrophe of his country than many other Russians. His employer, Minatom, Russia's Ministry of Atomic Energy, provided him with a decent apartment and better-than-average pay on those occasions when the checks did arrive.

Anatoly jumped when his quiet solitude was broken by the ringing of his black, rotary phone. He grabbed the handset and mumbled a greeting.

"This is Alexei Korgonyuk from Minatom Internal Security," the caller said. The gravelly voice was unfamiliar to Anatoly, and he tried to remember the few faces he'd seen from Internal Security. "There has been a serious breach of security here. We need your help to determine who may be responsible.

Anatoly's heart raced. The death penalty could be imposed for a security breach involving nuclear secrets. "I don't see how I could possibly help. I haven't seen any suspicious activity."

"Report to your office immediately, and we'll explain the situation when you arrive." Korgonyuk sounded impatient. "Do not discuss what you are doing with anyone. It may be that a fellow employee in your Minatom apartment building is involved."

Anatoly hung up the phone and stepped back to the table where he shoveled out a couple spoonfuls of meat and vegetables from his bowl and then slurped down the broth.

Anatoly did not suspect that his caller was a man on the *mafiya* payroll who had studied his comings and goings for more than a week. He had been followed to work every morning and home again in the evening. He was trailed to lunch and out with his friends on the previous Friday night. He didn't know his apartment had been searched and bugged and his phone tapped. He didn't know that a man watched him now as he ate.

A secretary in his office observed his habits at work. She didn't know why she was paid to report on such mundane things, but she didn't care. She needed the money to help support herself, her daughter and her ailing mother who lived with her.

Anatoly slipped on a beige trench coat with a thick lining to ward off the frigid winds continuing to blow in defiance of the calendar. He tromped down the steps of the apartment building and, once outside, walked on the familiar path toward the Kievsky train station. He traveled less than a half-block before the man with binoculars entered Anatoly's apartment building.

The stranger wore a medium-length, black leather coat and gloves and gray wool pants. He slipped his sunglasses into a breast pocket and ascended the stairs two at a time, his black running shoes allowing him to move quietly. He looked up and down the hallway, and put an ear to Anatoly's door. Hearing nothing inside, he inserted a lock pick in the door and worked it in and out as he twisted the lock cylinder with a narrow blade of steel. The lock yielded with a click.

The man slid into the apartment like a shadow. He shut the door without a sound and scanned the living room. A mix of furniture filled the room, a new matching sofa and chair accompanied by a beat-up rocker and an old coffee table. He was pleased to see a modern, black lacquered entertainment center with a 40-plus-inch flat-screen Swedish television and stereo system at the center of one wall—the presence of these items would make what he was about to deposit more believable.

He moved to the bedroom where he located a chest of drawers. He pulled a thick wad of U.S. twenty dollar bills and a package wrapped in brown paper from inside his coat and, with a gloved hand, nestled the items in a sock drawer.

As he pushed the drawer shut, he heard keys jingling in the hallway outside the apartment. He darted behind the bedroom door as Anatoly reentered the apartment. The stranger reached under his coat behind his back and yanked a Glock pistol from a Mossad four-way holster strapped horizontally to his belt. Through the gap along the doorjamb, he glimpsed Anatoly walk past the bedroom door, and his grip tightened on the gun. Beads of sweat oozed from his forehead, and he constricted his chest muscles, breathing shallowly.

Anatoly scooped up a file folder on an end table and walked past the bedroom door a second time. Then he exited the apartment.

The man listened motionless, counting to himself. He stepped from behind the door and peeked out a window. He couldn't see Anatoly, but not much of the sidewalk below was visible. The stranger strode across the apartment, listened at the door before opening it, and left.

Anatoly had much of the sidewalk to himself as he headed toward the office. It was Monday, and a state holiday fell on Wednesday of the week. Many people had taken advantage of the situation by extending their weekend to five days.

He descended the broad, concrete stairs into the Kievsky underpass to catch the subway. He failed to notice that a man appeared above him, reached beneath the lapel of a sport coat, and pulled out a dull charcoal pistol.

Halfway down the stairs, Anatoly's legs crumpled and his upper body hurtled forward unrestrained. His eyes widened with puzzlement in the instant of consciousness that remained. He tried to yell, but his lungs, filling with blood, could only gurgle. A shattered spine rendered his arms useless. His head slammed into the steps, his neck twisting grotesquely from the impact. Papers erupted from the folder and scattered. As his body slid further down, red streaks trailed behind.

The gunman watched with a blank face. He waited for the body to stop moving and then fired three shots at Anatoly's head, emptying the clip. He dropped the Glock 9mm with attached silencer, serial numbers filed off, and fled to the waiting white Zhiguli sedan. Gloves that had kept the gunshot residue off the shooter's hands were peeled off and discarded on the curb. The car, a common model on Moscow streets, blended into the other traffic and disappeared.

Timothy S. Jacobson

CHAPTER FIVE

Madison

"Let's put the bomb in the dumpster," Gene said.

"Shhh!" Kent replied. "You're gonna get us caught."

The two walked with short, quick steps in the dark alley, looking over their shoulders every few steps. Kent clutched the explosive device under his arm, inside his navy-blue, nylon ski jacket. The device had taken him a month to create in his spare time.

A siren wailed, and the pair jerked their heads around and froze. The sound grew louder.

"It's just a fire truck," Gene said. I can tell."

Kent paused a moment, wanting to be sure they were safe. Then he led on to the dumpster, grabbing the corner of its lid and flinging it back. The lid slipped out of his fingers and crashed against the brick wall behind it. Both boys cringed as the sound echoed out from the alley. Again, they paused and looked around.

"All clear," Gene whispered through clenched teeth.

Kent delicately rested the C-4 "shaped charge" on some garbage as he struggled to ignore the stench. One end of the explosive device featured a conical depression, and Kent pressed it against the side wall of the dumpster.

The shape of the bomb had been designed to focus the energy of blast to increase its ability to penetrate or "cut" through a solid structure. The C-4 had been manufactured by the teenagers from chemicals "borrowed" from a supply room at the university.

"How do these walkie-talkies work as a detonator anyway?" Gene asked while Kent fidgeted with the placement of the bomb.

Kent loved explaining his handiwork. "I attached a decoding circuit to the walkie-talkie connected to the bomb. It's the receiving unit. The decoding circuit detects and distinguishes the Morse Code tone generated when I press the tone button on the other walkie-talkie, which is the transmitting unit. When the tone is received, an electrical impulse is sent to the detonator."

Gene looked over the edge of the dumpster and studied the bomb. "Are you sure this thing won't go off before we get away?"

"Yes. I removed the battery from the transmitting unit before leaving home in case the walkie-talkie was accidentally turned on and the tone button pressed."

Gene squirmed. He shifted his weight from one foot to the other. "What about someone else setting it off with a walkie-talkie or a CB?"

Kent frowned. "It's not very likely that someone else is running around this neighborhood at this very moment carrying a walkie-talkie with a tone generator of the same frequency. And not too many CB's I know of have Morse

Code buttons. Ya know, you're starting to sound like my dad."

"I just don't want to get my head blown off."

They finished positioning the bomb and scurried out of the alley a mostly-abandoned corner of this old industrial part of the city. There were a few run-down apartment buildings scattered about, and a dog barked a few blocks away.

The boys saw no one around. Little traffic found its way down here, just an occasional big car old enough to be considered an antique but for the rust and bubbled paint.

Gene, holding the transmitting walkie-talkie, returned it to Kent for the honor of detonating the

C-4. More than happy to let Kent push the button, Gene could now honestly say, if they were caught, that he hadn't set off the beast.

The boys stuffed cotton in their ears and pressed their bodies against the brick walls of the buildings, one on each side of the alley.

Each craned his neck and peered down the alley one last time to make sure all was clear. Gene looked over at Kent so he would know when the bomb was about to go off.

Kent inserted the battery into the walkie-talkie and turned it on. He held his finger over the Morse Code button, paused for a moment, his muscles tensed. Gene looked away from Kent and put his hands over his ears. Kent glanced at Gene, then pushed the button.

The bomb detonated with a sharp, deafening noise, and a flash of light momentarily illuminated their surroundings. Pieces of debris flew out from the alley.

Gene and Kent waited for a couple seconds, then carefully looked around the corner with one eye each. A cloud of dust and smoke rolled out of the alley while scorched garbage rained from the sky. Nearby windows had shattered. They tried to see the damage to the dumpster, but the street light no longer worked, shrouding the alley in darkness.

"Awesome!" exclaimed Gene.

"Yes!" Kent shouted, gesturing with a downward stroke of his arm.

The dog stopped barking, then resumed with greater urgency, now joined by another dog. One seemed to be coming closer. A man's voice rang out from an apartment building down the street.

Gene and Kent ran to their mountain bikes, jumped on, and rode into a small, murky mix of woods and marsh. While they rode among the trees, losing the thin trail to darkness, sirens approached from two directions. Kent, in the lead, hit a bump he had forgotten about and almost skidded out of control on the muddy path. Gene's front tire spun against Kent's back wheel. He swerved to avoid a more serious collision and shot off into the marsh sedge and scattered bushes, putting Kent well ahead of him as he struggled to return to the trail.

The boys emerged on the other side of the woods into a modest, residential neighborhood where by pre-arrangement they split up to head to their respective homes.

"Talk to you tomorrow," Gene yelled.

Kent didn't respond, not wanting to attract attention. They both gasped for breath and sweated profusely as their legs furiously pumped the pedals. With each passing vehicle and pedestrian, both felt they were being watched, as if everyone knew what they had done.

Almost home, Gene spotted a squad car parked along the street. He wondered if it would raise suspicion to turn onto another street. I can't chance having them see me, he thought. At the last instant, he turned sharply to the right, and moments later, his circuitous path took him home. He saw his mother and stepfather watching TV through the living room window.

The smell of microwave popcorn struck his nostrils as he opened the door. No one acknowledged his arrival. He went upstairs to his bedroom and collapsed on the bed. After he caught his breath, he started flipping through a military supplies catalog. He was too wound-up to consider sleep.

Kent turned into his own driveway and shot into the garage. He sat on his bike in the dark, thinking, and listening to the sounds of the night and his own heavy breathing. The sweat had built up under his jacket, and a large, cool drop ran down from his armpit along his side. Kent felt proud of the successful detonation of a high-tech explosive device he had crafted by hand.

He heard a vehicle slowly approaching on the street. A patrol car rolled into view.

Kent's heart, which had started to slow when he arrived home, now began racing again. The car couldn't have been going more than five or ten miles per hour. The cop on the passenger side looked right up Kent's driveway. Kent sat very still and stopped breathing. His lungs burned: he hadn't caught his breath yet from the ride home. The car slowly passed out of view, and he resumed breathing, quick, deep breaths.

Kent waited until the cop car had cleared the block. Then he quietly got off his bike and put the kickstand down, and walked with a deliberately-normal pace into the house, not wanting to draw attention to himself.

During the night, Kent woke up dreaming that he had been identified by a witness to the bombing and that the police had arrested him. He saw a person lurking in the distance, but couldn't identify the face. He lay awake trying to convince himself he wouldn't be caught.

The next morning, Kent stumbled down the stairs and into the kitchen for breakfast. His dad sat at the table, reading the morning paper.

"Can you believe this?" the elder Dalton said. "Last night someone set off a bomb not far from here. Two kids were seen. Apparently it was a sophisticated device, some sort of plastic explosive with a radio-controlled detonator. The detonator got blown clear of the explosion largely intact."

Kent, wide-awake now, turned to the refrigerator to hide his nervousness. "Do they have any suspects?"

"It doesn't say, but it looks like they have some good leads. I wouldn't be surprised if they found the kids within a week."

CHAPTER SIX

Moscow
June

The tall man hunched over the computer screen, fixated on the scrolling text. The nails of his left hand were planted like roots in his scalp, sandy-brown hair drifting over the fingertips.

"Boris Levovich," came a voice from behind, causing him to jump.

Boris spun in his chair, doing his best to block the computer monitor. "Gennady Nikolayevich.

What's up?"

"I was just passing by. Sorry to startle you."

"I guess I'm tense because of the deadlines

I'm under."

"I've noticed you putting in long days. Hey, do you want to get some lunch?" Gennady asked.

"I'd love to, but I have to run some errands. Maybe tomorrow. We also need to finish our discussion about improving security procedures in our ministry."

"I'm tied up tomorrow morning, but maybe we can have lunch and then go through the security issues for a while in the afternoon."

Boris glanced at his calendar. "That should work with my schedule."

"Good. See you around." Gennady turned and walked toward the stairs, but he struck up a conversation with another employee a few cubicles away.

Boris exited the program on his computer and waited for Gennady to disappear, then left the Minatom building. He wove through the swarm of pedestrians on the sidewalk along the automobile-choked Tverskaya Ulitsa, his brow wrinkled in frustration from having to navigate around the numerous vendors in street kiosks. He squinted over his shoulder into the bright sunlight as he approached an intersection. He scanned faces before diving to the right down a twisted side street.

Taking long strides, he mumbled a curse when, out of the corner of his eye, he saw the gold Mercedes charge toward him. It pulled alongside and matched his pace as he continued walking. The car lurched ahead and stopped. The rear power window slid down, and the occupant in the back whistled. Boris turned with mock surprise and froze for a moment while he looked at his pursuer, Kirill Ivanovich Kardirov. Boris walked up to the car. A man came out of the front passenger seat and opened the back door.

Kardirov looked at his guest with great concern. "Boris Levovich, how are you? You've made yourself hard to reach lately."

The car started moving. Boris looked down at his hands, which he folded and unfolded. "I've been busy."

"Well, you've been making Nikolai Mikhailovich nervous. How are things in your new job at Minatom?"

Boris tried to control his breathing. "Are you sure it's a good idea for us to meet now? I don't want any suspicions raised."

"No one knows you're with me. You know we have sophisticated counter-surveillance. And if you're concerned about people looking into the unfortunate death of your predecessor at Minatom, it's all been taken care of. Our people at the police station confirmed that once the drugs and a significant amount of cash were found in Anatoly's apartment, the ministry was glad he died. They don't want a drug dealer in such a sensitive position." Kardirov smiled. "You can't trust a drug dealer, you know." His smile faded, and he took on a more serious expression. "You still haven't told me how things are."

Boris attempted a smile. "Fine, I guess. I just get a little paranoid sometimes."

"That's understandable. You do your part and remember who you work for, and everything will be alright. We will take care of you." Kardirov patted Boris on the shoulder.

"I'm meeting with Gennady Nikolayevich tomorrow, and I should learn more about security weaknesses," Boris said. "I'll need that information, because my progress with accessing classified information on the computer is slow."

"Gennady thinks he is discussing security with you to improve it when actually you're undermining it. I like that." Kardirov motioned to the driver to stop. "Keep in touch. If I have to come looking for you again, it will be through a rifle scope," Kardirov warned, raising his eyebrows. "If you have any problems at work, get out of there and call me. Just say you want to meet for lunch. If you say 'tomorrow,' I'll know you mean that same day."

Boris stepped out of the car and stooped down to look back in. "I will keep in touch." As the Mercedes sped away, Boris looked around and darted down the sidewalk.

CHAPTER SEVEN

Madison
Mid-July

This summer Kent Dalton had enrolled at the UW in an advanced computer science class and a course in western political philosophy. The computer class was easy enough— Kent had been programming computers since age eight.

The political philosophy course proved a little more challenging. The class, usually taken only by upperclassmen, studied Machiavelli now, and Kent couldn't get enough of it.

The professor looked over the class and turned to a student on his left. "Sarah, could you go to page 52 in *The Prince* and read the second full sentence?"

"Sure." Sarah flipped through her copy of the slim treatise and read:

> And many writers have imagined for themselves republics and principalities that have never been seen nor known to exist in reality; for there is such a gap between how one lives and how one ought to live that anyone who abandons what is done for what ought to be done learns his ruin rather than

his preservation: for a man who wishes to profess goodness at all times will come to ruin among so many who are not good. Hence it is necessary for a prince who wishes to maintain his position to learn how not to be good, and to use this knowledge or not to use it according to necessity.

Sarah stopped and looked up at the professor.

"Well Sarah, what do you think? Should a prince abandon what is done for what ought to be done?"

"It seldom happens, but I think that if our leaders worked harder at doing what they ought to do, we would have a better, more peaceful world."

"Does everyone agree with Sarah?" Kent raised his hand. "Yes, Kent," the professor said.

"I don't know. I don't see how governments can be totally up-front and honest all the time. For example, if the primary role of government is to provide stability and security to its citizens, a big part of deterring aggressor nations is to create disinformation about strengths and capabilities. Governments have to engage in covert operations and spy on other countries to do things like stopping nuclear proliferation. If the government was honest about everything it did, even if only to its own citizens, nothing could be done covertly."

The professor pointed his pen at Kent. "Do you see a problem of definition here, class? In other words, you are left to make assumptions about what is done versus what ought to be done? Also, in your example, Kent, haven't you made assumptions about the interactions of neighboring countries that might be altered in positive ways if each country chose to act as they 'ought to?' Maybe if governments were more open, there would be fewer misunderstandings and more cooperation."

"I don't know," a student interjected. "I kind of agree with Kent. It's like the song 'Fly Me Courageous' where it says 'Mother America is brandishing her weapons. She keeps me safe and warm by threats and misconceptions,'" the student sang. Laughter spread through the classroom.

The professor rolled his eyes. "Thank you for that insightful analysis."

After Kent's political philosophy class, he walked to a lab in the engineering building to work on the research project headed by his dad. John Dalton was working to develop an integrated system of devices to monitor brain wave and peripheral nerve activity in real time which they dubbed the "Multi-Input Physiological High-Speed Computer Interface," "MIPHSCI" for short. If the hardware could be integrated properly with sufficiently powerful software, there would be great potential for applications in limb prostheses control and virtual reality, not to mention the potential as a powerful analytical tool in many areas of physiological and psychological research.

When Kent walked into the lab, two graduate engineering students, Phil and Stan, were busy constructing the hardware interface connecting the output of various devices for measuring brain activity and nerve impulses to the computer system.

"Sit down Dr. Doogie Houser," Phil joked.

Stan grinned. "Yeah, we need a guinea pig for testing our electric chair."

Kent plopped down and reclined on the "bed" of the scanning device, which rode on a track to move Kent's head into the middle of a large, white ring. "Okay, fry me," he replied.

Phil and Stan hooked Kent up with more wires than a Christmas tree, except with electrodes instead of colored lights. Kent's brain blood flow was monitored by a positron emission tomographic scan to determine which regions had the highest metabolic activity, while simultaneous electroencephalograph and functional magnetic resonance imaging scans were performed. The movement of Kent's eyes were tracked by a low-power laser emitting light in an invisible part of the spectrum along with electrooculographic signal devices, and this information was used to control servos connected to a small, closed-circuit TV camera which allowed the computer to see what Kent saw. Audio input was derived from two microphones.

Stan flipped some switches after the electrodes were in place, but nothing happened. "He's brain dead!" Stan shouted with mock concern, placing the palms of his hands on the sides of his face like a character in an Edvard Munch painting.

Kent rolled his eyes. "If anyone's brain dead it's you, since you haven't got this thing working yet. Maybe you should try plugging it in over there."

"I don't know why I'm wasting so much time on this project," Phil complained in an abrupt change of subject, his tone flipping from humor to pessimism. "It's never going to work anyway. There's just no way a computer can process and integrate the output from all these devices in a meaningful way, and certainly not in real time. Even with much faster computers than we have now, it would take forever for the computer to sort through all the information, and by that time, the subject's activities and state of mind would have changed too much for the system to get any feedback and learn."

"Baloney," countered Kent. "All you need is a large enough neural net, enough input, and enough training sessions, and soon the computer will be functioning like a second brain. This project has the potential to be a lot more than fancy VR gear."

"You're both full of shit," Stan said. "We'll get something useful out of this project, but it certainly isn't going to be a 'second brain.'" Turning to Kent, Stan said, "I just can't understand how people like you can believe in artificial intelligence. You ought to read Roger Penrose's books sometime. He's a leading scholar on the subject, and he's got an interesting theory on how the human brain can never be duplicated by a computer—something to do with the way the brain functions at the quantum mechanical level."

"Stan, you don't know what you're talking about," Kent shot back. "Penrose has sipped too many cups of tea at Oxford. He makes all sorts of ridiculous assumptions to reach an absurd conclusion about why technology will never be able to match the human brain. The brain does some pretty amazing things, but like everything, its processes will eventually be reduced to simple rules that can be used to duplicate its functions. The brain is nothing more than a certain arrangement of chemicals and electrical impulses."

Stan scowled, but Kent continued, "It's like when I was a little kid and saw a Rubic's Cube. At first, I thought there could be arrangements in which the cube was unsolvable. Then at some point I realized that since the cube started in an ordered state and became 'mixed-up' through a series of twists and turns, the cube could always be reorganized by reversing the steps which messed it up no matter how convoluted and complex it was.

"Likewise, the brain starts out as an essentially blank or ordered state, which gets mixed-up, twisted, and kinked in the learning process. There is nothing magical about the brain. It's a physical system that learns through physical stimuli. It's naive to think that just because our attempts to create artificial intelligence have had very limited success so far, we will never be able to mimic the brain's ability to understand and reason. Every concrete problem in the physical world is solvable. You just need enough information about it—identify the operational units and the rules by which they behave. Even if we accept Penrose's idea that brain function is dependent on quantum states, then we will just have to duplicate the brain structures in which quantum gravity supposedly operates. Flying isn't just for birds anymore, you know."

Stan put his hand to his chin and stroked his three-day-old stubble. "I still think you're full of shit."

CHAPTER EIGHT

Miami

"I would like to close my account," Leonard Korshakov said, sliding a piece of paper across the private banker's desk. "The top number is my account here; the bottom one is where I'd like the money transferred."

"I'm sorry to hear you're leaving us," said the middle-aged woman. She looked at Korshakov hoping for an explanation.

Korshakov returned the gaze, unblinking. He thought about the details of completing his escape from employment under Nikolai Volkov. He wished he could disappear as quickly and easily as the laundered drug money about to be transferred.

The banker pivoted to her computer and entered the account number. She kept her reaction hidden when the balance of more than one and a half-million dollars appeared on the screen. "You want the entire amount transferred?"

"Yes, all of it."

"I'm sorry, but I need to see identification."

Korshakov presented a false driver's license with the same name he used to open the account.

The woman studied the license for a moment, then scratched out the account number and balance on a wire slip and set it in front of Korshakov. "Please sign the transfer authorization." He signed the alias without pause.

After leaving the bank, Korshakov crawled into his Lincoln Town Car and drove to the small office that served as the front for the laundering operations. Inside, he sat at his desk, pulled a handgun from his shoulder holster, removed a silencer from a desk drawer, and screwed the black cylinder onto the gun barrel. He placed the pistol in his lap and called his partner, Dimitri, on the phone, asking him to come to the office immediately.

Dimitri lived ten minutes away. Korshakov busied himself with the newspaper while he waited. When Dimitri arrived, he folded the paper and tossed it on the floor.

"What's wrong?" Dimitri asked.

"What's wrong is I'm sick of taking orders from Nikolai Volkov. We send him huge amounts of cash and see little of it ourselves. The Colombians don't care much for him and his cut either. We have an opportunity to continue working with the Colombians for ourselves. Are you interested?"

"You're crazy. He'll kill you." While Dimitri had certainly entertained thoughts about breaking free from Volkov, it had been merely idle daydreaming to him. Korshakov's proposition shocked him.

"Volkov's network is very limited here, and he exerts no direct control in Colombia. You know we have been running this operation by ourselves."

"What about our families in Russia?" Dimitri nervously wiped sweat from his brow.

"What about them? You can pick up a fine señorita in Colombia and start a new family."

"No, this is madness."

"I'm sorry it has to be this way, Dimitri. I hoped I wouldn't have to do this alone."

Korshakov reached toward the gun on his lap. Dimitri instinctively reached for his own pistol and pulled it from the holster before the simmering lead struck him, first in the side of the neck, then in the abdomen. He dropped his handgun and fell to his knees, staring incredulously at Korshakov, who rose from his chair and extended his arm to move the muzzle closer to Dimitri's head. Dimitri looked down at the blood-soaked hands holding his belly, then rolled his eyes upward to Korshakov just before two bullets entered his skull.

Korshakov wrapped the body in an old blanket and dragged it to a closet. He mopped up the blood with paper towels and flushed them down the toilet.

At nightfall, he drove his Lincoln up to the back door, unscrewed the light bulb above the steps, and lugged his former partner into the steamy night air. He struggled to lift the body into the trunk, getting the upper half in first, then strained to get the feet in.

He wove the Lincoln through the city, along streets he'd become familiar with in four years of pretending to be an American. He exited a residential neighborhood and picked up I-95 North. After twenty minutes, he headed south. Back in the city of Miami proper, he left the freeway to wind along residential areas, and eventually got on U.S. 41, driving west into the Everglades. Dimitri will make good alligator food, Korshakov thought.

After disposing of the body in a swamp, he returned to the city where he would spend one last night before flying to Colombia from Miami International Airport. He would have preferred to leave immediately, and was ready to do so, but had built extra time into his plans to allow for difficulties, and his Colombian contact would not be ready to receive him until the following day. It would be a long wait.

CHAPTER NINE

Madison

Kent sat at the kitchen table eating dinner with his father, the sound of forks and knives clinking on the china as they ate in silence. John was absorbed in reviewing budget reports for his department at the university.

Kent finished his meal and rinsed off his plate. "Dad, I'm going to stay over at Gene's tonight. Is that okay?"

"Sure, that's fine. Just be back in the afternoon. I'm going to need your help fixing the bathroom sink."

Kent frowned. "Yes, Dad." He went out to the garage to get his bike to go to the university. He had no intention of going to Gene's. He'd told his father he was spending the night so no one would check on him.

As Kent rolled his bike out of the garage into the steamy summer air, Kim, a female classmate of his who lived two houses away, stepped out her front door in shorts and a T-shirt and bounded down the steps toward her boyfriend's red MX-5 Miata convertible.

"Hi, Kent!" she shouted.

"Hi, Kim." He mustered a smile.

She let herself into the car, and Kent sat on his bike and watched as they drove away. He stared unblinking at the road even after the Miata had disappeared. He thought about when he and Kim had been in grade school together. They'd seemed inseparable—riding their bikes down the sidewalk side-by-side, playing in the nearby park on the swings and slide, giggling in class.

He wondered when they'd drifted apart. Maybe it started when Kent's mother, Lucille, died. Lucille had often taken them places together. After her death, Kim seemed to withdraw, unsure how to respond—or had Kent drawn into himself? Maybe their interests diverged after the Daltons bought their first home computer and Kent spent hours playing games and learning how to write programs.

"Kent, you're still here?"

Kent turned to see his father standing on the front steps. "Uh, yeah. I'm heading out now. See ya."

John cocked his head and raised one eyebrow as Kent pedaled out of the driveway. "Have a good night."

Kent mumbled an acknowledgment and rode off toward Gene's house, then changed direction and headed toward the university.

Kent was still thinking about Kim when he arrived at Sewart Hall. He shoved his bike into the bike rack and walked away without locking it up. Not until he sat down at the keyboard and began to work did his thoughts turn to MIPHSCI and his desire to create an intelligent, anticipatory neural interface. He knew that to get the hardware to accomplish his goal, he needed heretofore unattained computing power.

He also knew his father had more modest goals for this research project. The best-case scenario, as Prof. Dalton saw it, involved producing either a commercially viable system of limited analytical power, or something the military would find interesting and continue funding. Prof. Dalton also assumed that the process of creation would provide a good learning environment for his students and himself.

Kent's goals were not so confined, because he was willing to consider means of obtaining computing power which were not legal. He believed the key to creating a truly intelligent device lay in harnessing a vast network of computers, all contributing a fraction of their processing power.

The problem Kent faced involved how to obtain the use of hundreds or even thousands of computers for his project. The solution had to include hacking into countless university, corporate, military, and government computers to utilize their resources.

Breaking into isolated computers posed little problem for Kent. He had done it on and off for several years just for fun. The real challenge would be gaining access to a large number of computers that he could call upon simultaneously while avoiding detection. This required techniques he had not previously employed, and even once he had access, he needed to write special software to coordinate the transfer of data among computers.

Kent set about the task of making MIPHSCI work. The lab lay deathly quiet, with just the faint hum of computer cooling fans. Even the most dedicated college students were taking a break, busy unwinding on this Friday evening.

Kent began by reviewing and updating some previous "research" he had performed on the topic of hacking methods. He read over some computer files he had downloaded from the Internet describing various computer security weaknesses. Some of the information came from hackers and security experts who exchanged ideas by posting messages in e-mail discussion groups, including BUGTRAQ, and other material he gathered from Web sites devoted to hacking.

It seemed everyone stood ready to share their expertise on how to outsmart the computer security experts. Hackers inundated Kent with information, a lot from people who thought they knew more than they actually did.

Late on the following Saturday morning, Kent called Gene from home and told Gene to meet him at the lab in Sewart Hall where he would be programming.

After both arrived, Kent unlocked the lab door and they went in.

"So what exactly are we going to do anyway?" Gene asked.

"We gotta get the program done to gain access to large numbers of computer systems for MIPHSCI."

"I know that, but how are we going to write one program that can gain access to different kinds of systems?"

"Often, when a computer system is installed, it has a few easy means of access, such as a standard username and password meant to be changed right after setup. Lax system operators don't always get around to closing these holes. Other systems have tighter security, but no system is impenetrable."

"I don't think you're going to get into as many systems as you'd like," Gene said.

"It's not going to be perfect, but we need to write a program that will automatically probe thousands of computer systems for weaknesses. Unfortunately, we can't use the same technique as Robert Morris, Jr.—he's the graduate student who created the 'worm' that brought the Internet to its knees a number of years ago—the SMPT vulnerability he used has been fixed. Our program will be designed so that when it finds a point of entry into a computer system, it will establish access to that system, taking as much control as possible. Then it will record the information necessary to get back in and move on to another computer system. Each computer that is taken over will be enlisted to take over more systems, resulting in a geometric increase in the number we have access to. We'll have the program designed to run in the background without the need of our supervision."

Gene looked at Kent with skepticism. "What about firewalls? How are you going to penetrate those?"

"Obviously, when a computer firewall is encountered, more elaborate steps will have to be taken to penetrate it. You've watched me get through before."

"Okay, so once we've established this group of computers awaiting our command, how do we use that to process the information from MIPHSCI?"

"We'll build a neural network. You know what that is, don't you?"

"I've heard of 'em, but I guess I really don't know how they work."

"Each computer will act as part of a larger neural network, essentially a collection of 'neurons' connected by 'synapses' that exist only as equations in the computer program and change their values in response to input from surrounding neurons. A software neuron has no *mind* of its own, but merely fires in response to stimuli in the form of input from adjacent neurons. It's kinda like the collective abilities of thousands of mindless ants conducting discrete, small tasks that together result in a complex environment of tunnels which allows the colony to be sustained and to grow."

"This is going to eat up some serious lines of code."

"I know. That's why I called you to help."

"Can't we find a way to exploit all the PC's on the Internet? Then instead of thousands of computers working for us, we'd have millions."

Kent thought for a moment and then raised his eyebrows. "That might work. Windows allows resource sharing. On each larger computer system we crack, we can periodically issue the 'netstat' command to determine the IP addresses assigned to PC's when they connect. Then for each IP address we identify, we'll use the 'nbtstat' command to check the NetBIOS remote machine name table to see which machines have file sharing enabled. Then it's a piece of cake to take control."

"I bet there's a ton of users who stay online for hours or days at a time," Gene said, "which would allow us time to pin down the addresses and squeeze some CPU time out of them. If we could get an hour of CPU time for each of a few million PC's every day in addition to a thousand larger computer systems, that would be friggin' awesome."

Kent went over his detailed algorithm, essentially an outline of the tasks the program would perform, explaining it to Gene. Then they divided up certain tasks. The pair slugged away for several hours working on the program.

Later, Gene stopped what he was doing, got up from his chair, and stretched with a big yawn. He walked over to the window and looked out at the surrounding campus. "Kent, doesn't it concern you that we're going to try to break into all these computers?"

"What? You mean if we get caught, or just whether it's right or wrong?"

"I don't know. Either."

"Well, I'd be stupid if the thought hadn't passed through my mind. Of course it's illegal, but I'm writing the program carefully to prevent getting caught. I guess the bigger question is whether it's right. It's not going to hurt anything, so I don't see what's the big deal. I intend to create something that ultimately will be valuable to society. I'm not going to destroy other people's data or disrupt computer systems in such a way as to prevent others from using them. I'm merely going to use a fraction of the resources of any given system. Once I've proven my ideas are viable, I'll have a basis for seeking more legitimate means of continuing the project. Haven't you ever read the frequently asked questions for alt.2600?"

Gene turned away from the window. "The FAQ for the hacking newsgroup? I skimmed it once a while back."

"It has a statement about the ethics of computer hacking. It says something about access to computers—and anything that might teach you about the way the world works—should be unlimited and total. Always yield to the 'hands-on imperative.' It also says all information should be free, you should mistrust authority and promote decentralization. That's what we're doing."

CHAPTER TEN

Kaliningrad, Russia

"Leonard Korshakov is missing along with about $1.6 million." Kirill Kardirov paused for a moment, his wrinkled brow contorting his birthmark. "We think he made some good friends from Colombia while in Florida. It'll be difficult to get to him there. He'll be well protected." Kardirov's knuckles turned white as he gripped the phone, waiting to pull it away from his ear if necessary.

Kardirov's *mafiya* boss, Nikolai Mikhailovich Volkov, snapped ashes from his cigarette toward the marble ashtray on the large, messy desk of the Russian oil company executive he visited. "Where's his partner?" Volkov whispered into the phone, his face reddening.

"He's gone too. I sent someone down to check out the office, and he found blood. Wouldn't have noticed if he hadn't been looking for it. It matches the blood type from Dimitri's military records."

"I wouldn't have expected Dimitri to be part of this. What's left of our operation?"

"We're going to have to start over."

"Korshakov has a family, doesn't he?"

"Yes, a wife and a boy. We just checked on them. They're still in St. Petersburg."

Volkov had been born in St. Petersburg, called Leningrad at the time, and he knew the city intimately. The *mafiya* boss' thoughts turned for an instant to the days of his childhood, playing along the majestic, fast-flowing River Neva that divided the city into north and south.

Volkov's days of innocence had not lasted long. At age eight, he knew there were things his father, Mikhail, did of which he could never speak, even though he didn't understand why.

At twelve, his family moved to Moscow. Nikolai was the oldest of three children, and his father enlisted him as a courier for black market trans-actions. Nikolai didn't grasp the seriousness of what he did.

Mikhail had always been quick to praise Nikolai when he completed a job, rewarded him with treats, and the son developed a deep respect for his father. Then one night came a knock on the door, and Mikhail got led away to prison.

Volkov's thoughts returned to the present, and he ground the remainder of his cigarette into the ashtray. "Eliminate his wife. Do it publicly. It probably will have little effect on Korshakov, since he left them behind, but it sends a message to others."

"Yes, boss."

"While I have you on the phone, I might as well talk about this oil deal. We're having a real problem with some damn regulatory issues, particularly moving the stuff through multiple republics. Get Umov here next week. He's a genius when it comes to energy issues and red tape. Have him work with Stoletov."

"I think Stoletov has a full schedule next week."

"Well, bring him here. We need to keep the oil and the money flowing."

Kardirov hung up the phone and sighed. For a long time, he'd carried out Volkov's wishes without question or hesitation. Even murder had seemed justified: survival of the fittest—either walk on people or be walked upon. Kardirov didn't intend to be walked upon.

And yet, maybe another way existed. Kardirov saw legitimate business opportunities he could pursue, if only he had time. He wished he had a family, but didn't want to raise kids under his present circumstances. And the type of woman who might be attracted to a gangster such as himself was not necessarily the type of woman he'd want to marry.

He needed to complete one last big job being planned by Volkov. With his share of the money, Kardirov could start his own business, even several businesses, and break out of the rut he was in. He'd be able to think about settling down. He wasn't getting any younger, after all.

Kardirov daydreamed for several more minutes before picking up the phone and calling one of Volkov's killers. "I've got a job for you," he said. "It should be an easy one."

Timothy S. Jacobson

CHAPTER ELEVEN

Madison
Early October

A month had gone by since the start of the fall semester. Kent received a request in the mail from the university to act as a tutor for one or more students in the introductory computer science class. The university would pay him by the hour as work-study.

Oh great, Kent thought. Nothing worse than a geek-wannabe who can't handle some simple Pascal programming.

He decided to take on the job because he needed the money and it would be relatively easy work. He dropped the acceptance form back in the mail. A few days later he received a hastily scribbled note from a computer science professor stating that Kent would be tutoring a student named Sam Trzebiatowski.

"What the hell kind of name is that!" he exclaimed under his breath.

The note further said that the first tutoring session would be held in room 418 in the Computer Science Department on the following Tuesday at 7:00 p.m.

St. Petersburg, Russia

Nina Korshakov pulled clothes from the dryer and folded them on the couch in her living room in front of the TV. She was affluent enough to have new, modern appliances, but not enough of the *mafiya* money made it home to allow her a housekeeper to do this mundane work.

On those rare occasions when her husband, Leonard, stopped at home from his travels abroad, he always pulled up in an expensive car, a different one each time it seemed, and invariably, he would be dressed in a nice, new suit. When she dared challenge him about why the allowance he gave her and their three-year-old son was so small in comparison to the value of his cars and suits, he would scream at her, putting his reddening face inches from hers, about not being thankful for what he provided, saying the cars and fancy clothes were necessary for the work he did. You have to spend money to make money, he said.

As she folded a sheet, she thought about how much time she spent alone in their bed. Although the frequent physical separation from her husband had been going on for only a little more than a year, the emotional separation was longer standing. She knew her husband's distant attitude had been formed around the time she became pregnant with their son. When Leonard found out about the pregnancy, he asked Nina to get an abortion, not an uncommon procedure in Russia. When she refused, he did not speak to her for weeks.

As he withdrew his attention from her over time, she, in turn, withdrew from him, detaching herself emotionally. It was too painful to love him now.

She got up from the couch and walked over to an end table upon which her wedding photo rested. She picked it up by the edges of the frame and held it at arm's length, squinting at the image as if to see beyond the two dimensional picture into the realm of thought and emotion. She wiped the corner of her left eye, abruptly set the picture down, and walked back to the pile of clean laundry.

She did not suspect she was being studied through binoculars from the apartment building across the street, nor did she realize her movements were being monitored twenty-four hours per day to determine her habits so that the best time and place for her murder could be ascertained.

Madison

When Tuesday rolled around, Kent went to the university right after eating dinner so he could work on the MIPHSCI project prior to the tutoring session. While there, he became absorbed in debugging a software routine and forgot about tutoring until about 7:15. He grudgingly rose from his seat in front of his computer workstation and wandered over to the appointed meeting place.

It won't hurt Mr. Trzshitski or whatever his name is to wait a bit, Kent thought. I'm the teacher now.

Kent walked into room 418, empty except for a gorgeous female student with long, blonde, wavy hair and a hot body evident through her pink, clingy knit blouse and tight blue jeans. Kent stared at her.

The young woman abruptly looked up from the book she read. Kent averted his eyes to pretend he had been looking at the bulletin board on the wall, but then returned his gaze to her.

"Uh, you haven't seen some guy named Sam around here, have you?" Kent asked.

"You must be Kent," she replied.

"Uh. . . ."

"I'm Sam, but I'm not a guy." She picked up her bookmark and slipped it in the book, snapping it shut. "My name is Samantha, but I always go by Sam."

"Oh, I'm sorry. I thought, uh . . . ." Kent cut himself off. "Sorry I'm late. Why don't we get started?"

"Good idea. You're apparently as smart as you are punctual. Do you know what we're covering in class right now?"

"No," he answered, letting the insult slip by because of his embarrassment. "Why don't I have you tell me what you've covered so far this semester and what it is you need help with?"

"Well, we've gone over a lot of the basics. We learned about creating algorithms, then converting that to pseudocode and finally writing the programs in Pascal. We've studied flow-of-control statements, various input and output commands, and how to break computing tasks down into procedures."

Sam looked past Kent for a moment at the wall behind him, and then returned her gaze to him. "It's a little bit embarrassing having a tutor for this," she said, now feeling humble herself. "I get good grades, and it's not that I don't understand the concepts, but I have trouble implementing the stuff when we have to do longer programs. My grade in this class is in a nosedive."

"You don't need to be embarrassed about it. A lot of people have trouble programming."

"I don't see how anyone can ever get the hang of it."

"It helps if you have a genuine interest. If you spend a lot of time programming, it becomes natural just like spoken language."

"I guess that's part of my problem—I don't have a genuine interest."

"Why are you taking the class then?"

"I'm a marketing major. I thought that with the importance of computers and the Internet these days, some knowledge of programming would look good on my resume."

Kent nervously worked with Sam for a half hour. Then she abruptly closed her book and announced, "I've had enough programming for one day. Why don't you come over to my dorm room for the session next week? I've got a computer there, and my room is more comfortable than having to work in this lab."

"Sure."

"I'm in Smith Hall, room 209. Do you know where that is?"

"Yeah, I've been by there a lot. Never been inside though."

"I'll see you next Tuesday then," Sam said as she got up and headed for the door.

"I'll try not to keep you waiting next time."

That night, Kent did not get anything else accomplished. He called Gene and told him about the babe he was tutoring. "Man, she even invited me to her place next week!"

"Cool. Don't do anything I wouldn't do—ha ha. And don't forget to wear clean underwear."

"Oh, shut up," he replied. "This tutoring thing is going to be great; next Tuesday Sam will be mine." While he talked with an air of confidence, inside he was terrified.

"Just give me a full report afterwards," Gene said with anticipation.

St. Petersburg

Nina Korshakov awoke early. Usually, she slept soundly until nine or nine-thirty in the morning. This night, however, she found herself looking at the clock numerous times and struggled to return to sleep. When she awoke at seven, she tried again to fall asleep, but after lying in bed awake for forty minutes, she decided to get up.

She was not surprised over her difficulty sleeping. An employee from their bank had called the previous day insisting that he speak with her husband as soon as possible. She had waited until evening to call Leonard because of the time zone difference. She started to worry when calling her husband's number in Florida yielded a recorded disconnect notice. She decided to wait a day to see if he would call her with a new number.

She went to the kitchen and made a pot of coffee. She took a cup when it was done and sipped it as she flipped through one of the many tabloids so popular now in Russia.

This morning, no one watched Nina for the first time in several days. No need existed—her routine had been ascertained.

After her son, who she lovingly referred to as Vovochka, awoke, she cooked oatmeal for his breakfast. Then she slipped on her exercise clothes and strapped the boy into the car. They drove to the sitter's apartment, the small but tidy home of an old woman.

From there, Nina drove to the health club, a modern facility located in a former warehouse. A small stream, obscured by a blanket of trees and bushes, meandered by the parking lot. Nina exited the car, gym bag in hand.

The bullet skimmed silently over the sea of car roofs, the pop from the silencer having been further muffled by the sound of traffic. A distraction caused Nina to turn just before the hollow-point projectile struck her.

The fortuitous movement of her body allowed her a few seconds of consciousness before death enveloped her. She felt no pain, but the darkness was immediate. Her pulse surged once in her ears and then faded. As her body crumpled, she sensed what had happened and attributed it to Leonard. Two other thoughts, feelings really, gelled in her mind before it expired: why had she chosen to marry Leonard, and what would become of her precious son?

Madison

Over the ensuing week, Kent uncharacteristically fretted about what to wear, what to say, and what to do at the next tutoring session. When Tuesday arrived, he woke up a half-hour before his alarm went off. He took a shower and spent extra time in the bathroom giving his longish hair a controlled, messy look.

He rode his bike to campus for his second political philosophy class. He strode across the sea of grass toward Boerner Hall. Even though he had gotten out of bed early, he was now running late. Waves of students carrying backpacks flooded across the lawn in front of him, rolling one way and another.

As he swept his eyes across this maze of moving obstacles, he caught sight of someone recognizable. Sam. She was walking on the sidewalk on the far side of this open area. He started toward her but, not wanting to seem too eager, changed course and headed to Boerner Hall.

Usually attentive in his political philosophy class, Kent was now distracted. He doodled in the margins of his notebook with a blank look on his face, his chin resting on one hand. He ignored the debate between the professor and one of the students about St. Augustine's rejection of pacifism and antimilitarism. Class seemed to take much longer than usual.

After class, Kent rode a city bus to his high school where Gene located him in the hall. Kent did not feel like talking right then, but knew no way existed to avoid him.

"Tonight's the big night!" Gene exclaimed. "Can I come with you?"

"You know, it's really not a big deal," Kent said as he buried his face in his locker digging for books. "It's just a tutoring session," Kent went on, not knowing what to expect from the evening with Sam, and trying to lower Gene's expectations.

"I know it's just tutoring, but the question is, who's tutoring who, and what's the subject?"

The day dragged on for Kent. He was frustrated by still being a high school student, at that awkward age of feeling adult-like but with a child's restrictions.

Having a taste of college life made him more impatient with his situation.

"Perhaps the problems which plagued the Weimar Republic can be explained by Mr. Dalton," Kent's history teacher said in response to Kent's obvious daydreaming.

"I'm sorry, I didn't hear the question," Kent replied, snapping out of his trance.

"Perhaps you should pay attention."

Kent arrived at Sam's dorm at 6:58 p.m. He did not want to be late like the last time, but didn't intend to show up too early either. He walked between the large, white columns at the top of the steps and entered the old, red brick building.

Entering the second floor hallway, he noticed two pairs of intertwined legs, one clad in blue jeans, the other belonging to a woman, and bare as far as what he could see of them, jutting out from the lounge halfway down the hall. Giggling noises emanated from the lounge, which he strained to hear over various types of music rumbling under doors.

As he looked for room 209, he stumbled over a pizza box. The smell of stale beer hung in the air. One of the fluorescent lights on the hallway ceiling flickered erratically; another had burned out.

When he found the room, he hesitated for a moment before knocking softly on the door. He heard music playing inside and a muffled voice. No answer. He knocked again. The dead bolt clicked open, and he smiled to greet Sam: instead a chubby young woman with straggly hair loomed in the doorway. Kent's smile faded. Maybe he had the wrong room.

"Is Sam here?" he asked.

"She's on the phone—come in. I'm Helen, her roommate."

"Yeah, yeah, I'll see ya later," Sam said into the phone in an irritated voice. "I've gotta go—my computer tutor is here—bye." She turned toward Kent with a forced grin on her face. "How ya doing?"

"Uh, good."

Clearly Sam came from an affluent family. Her dorm room walls were decorated with large, framed artwork, and she had an expensive stereo system with a large CD collection. An endless supply of clothes hung in the open closet area with rows of boxed shoes below, neatly arranged. She had a large aquarium with angel fish darting about inside. A small Persian-type rug covered the floor by her bed. Helen's side of the room was orderly and tasteful, but her furnishings and clothing were not as expensive as Sam's.

"Would you like a beer?" Sam asked.

"Sure." Kent hadn't yet developed much of a liking for beer, but he thought it might make him more relaxed. Besides, at 17, the last thing he'd do was turn down a beer. Sam opened her mini-fridge and pulled out two bottles of Ex Light.

"This okay?"

"Yeah, great."

"Here, sit down on my futon." She walked over to the stereo and turned down the volume on Ace of Base. Then she walked back over by Kent and plopped down beside him. "You look kind of young. What year are you in?"

Kent's face grew warm and he thought about lying. "Actually, I'm not enrolled full time. I'm only 17 and still finishing up my senior year of high school, but they let me take classes here."

"Wow, that's cool," Sam responded reassuringly.

Sam booted up her computer. "I need to have you help me with this program we're supposed to write to calculate commissions on securities transactions. Whenever someone selects one of the menu items, the whole thing goes berserk."

Kent looked over the source code of the program and found the main problems. While he explained them to Sam, he made the corrections himself without requiring her to figure out how to implement the solution. Kent hoped that by doing so, Sam would like him better. She didn't seem to mind having Kent do the work for her.

After Kent left, Helen said, "*High school.* He's still in high school?"

Sam shrugged her shoulders. "I knew he was young, but I didn't think of high school. He's not Orlando Bloom, but he's sorta cute, don't you think?"

"Yeah, I guess."

Sam fell back on her bed and looked up at the ceiling. "Something about those mischievous eyes."

Helen wagged a finger at her. "Watch it now. He's not even legal."

Sam looked at Helen and wrinkled her brow. "I didn't say I was going to sleep with him or even date him for that matter. He's definitely going to be my ticket to success in this computer class, though."

CHAPTER TWELVE

Moscow

"Boris, you're not making fast enough progress," Kirill Kardirov insisted on the phone to his "mole" in Minatom. "Nikolai Volkov's patience is wearing thin. We need the details of the nuclear consolidation *now*. It doesn't do any good for you to provide us with copies of encrypted e-mail messages we can't read."

"When I replaced Anatoly, I ended up with a low security clearance. That, plus limited time in front of the computer, impede my efforts," Boris Levovich whispered into the pay phone.

"We have to overcome those hurdles. Go to your office tonight and install the remote interface in your computer."

"There's too great a risk they'll discover the transmissions, and if not that, then the pattern of activity from my computer." Boris clamped one hand onto the top of his head as if to hold it together. "I just need a little more time."

"Time is up, Boris. Besides, we've minimized the risks. Our electrician rearranged the connections on the patch panel by the server. It would take them a while to pin down your machine if they became suspicious. And running the control signals through the building's electrical grid will be undetectable—the electrician already installed the signal amplification system. Call me from a different pay phone when you complete the task. We want to start our computer attacks before morning."

Boris walked up to the Minatom headquarters under a moonless night sky. He patted the breast pocket of his suit coat to reassure himself that he had not lost the contents.

He looked away to hide his face as a taxi passed him while he walked on the sidewalk. He scanned his surroundings upon reaching the main entrance of the Minatom building, then turned and walked up to the door. He produced a black plastic item on his key chain, about the size of a pack of gum, and held it up to a pad on the wall. A moment later, the green glow from an LED told him the door was unlocked. He walked through two sets of doors and was greeted by a middle-aged security guard.

"Back for more fun?" the guard joked.

"Yeah, it's too bad I don't have a twin to help me cover the long hours, but then there'd be two of us not getting paid."

The guard laughed as he looked at the Minatom ID badge Boris flashed at him, then jerked his head to the side to wave Boris in.

Boris walked down the corridor to the elevators. Once inside, he pressed the black plastic key onto a pad before he could select the third floor where
he worked.

The elevator opened into another corridor lined with doors with clear glass windows. Boris looked both ways and sighed when he confirmed that no lights were on. He went to the door leading to his office area and punched a seven-digit code on a keypad. The code unlocked the door and registered Boris as the person entering.

He flipped on the lights and walked to his cubicle near the middle of the large room. He pulled a small, leather-bound address book out of his breast pocket and rested it carefully on his desk. As he faced his desk, his back was to the door, and he turned every few seconds to see if anyone was walking down the corridor.

He lifted the computer monitor from the top of the CPU case and set it on the desk. He dug a screwdriver out of his desk drawer and pulled the computer case toward himself. Again, he looked over his shoulder at the door. After opening the case, he picked up the address book and unfastened the clasp. An interface card emerged from a thin, spongy sheet of packing material.

Boris whipped his head around when the elevator bell pierced the tomblike silence of the office. His heart raced as he stuffed the interface card back into the address book without the protective wrapping and replaced the computer case. He reached for the monitor but froze when he saw a woman's face peering in the door window. Boris vaguely recognized her as someone who worked farther down the hall in a different department. Boris nodded to the woman. She nodded in return and continued down the hall.

Boris waited several minutes and then wandered past the door, stealing glances into the hallway. Seeing no one, he returned to his desk and installed the interface card. He ran a wire from the card through the back of the computer and connected the loose end to a device on the desk that appeared to be an electric coffee cup warmer. Boris had brought the "cup warmer" to work weeks earlier; it served as the signal generator to transmit computer data through the electrical system.

He put the computer back together, exited the building, and headed out for a drink to calm his nerves.

Madison

When Kent wasn't spending time with Sam or thinking about her, he toiled to complete MIPHSCI, neglecting his other studies while staying up late night-after-night programming and testing subroutines.

Although Gene's programming skills were limited, Kent enlisted his help whenever he could. While Kent spent time conceptualizing and coming up with algorithms, Gene keyed in some of the code. Gene also made runs to pick up food and Mountain Dew to hold them over on late nights of programming.

Kent and Gene soon completed one of the major software components, and were ready to test their hacking tool for gaining access to large numbers of computer systems. It would be more difficult to write the software to interpret the human physiological data, but that software could not even be tested until a large network of computers stood by to process the information.

Kent and Gene waited until 1:30 on a Saturday morning to perform the first test. They wanted to try it when their activities would least likely be monitored.

"Alright, it should be ready to go," Kent said happily but with some apprehension.

"I sure hope you got this figured out," Gene said. "I don't want to go to jail."

"Stop worrying. This isn't the first time we've broken into other computers."

"That was different—we never did more than one at a time. Now we have a greater chance to get caught."

"Leave if you don't want to be around."

"No, I'll. . ."

"Here goes. This should be great!" Kent ran the program and inputted a number of parameters. When he typed the last parameter, he raised his right hand high with his index finger pointing down, paused for a moment, then jabbed at the "Enter" key with a flourish. The screen cleared, then flashed the status message "ATTEMPTING TO CONNECT 127.0.0.1." However, after several minutes when the status message failed to change, Kent grew suspicious and halted the program.

"Why did you do that?" Gene asked.

"Something's not right." Kent pulled up the source code with the text editor and scrolled down to a subroutine.

"Damn! That's why it wouldn't work," Kent said. He keyed in some changes, saved the revised source code and recompiled it.

"Is it going to work now?" Gene asked. Kent didn't answer, but proceeded to run the program again.

"ATTEMPTING TO CONNECT 127.0.0.1," the monitor displayed again. A moment later a new message appeared:

"CONNECTED TO 127.0.0.1."

Gene cracked a smile.

"We're not in yet," Kent cautioned.

Various messages scrolled up and off the screen while the program attempted to establish an account on the other computer, which could then be accessed quickly at any time. The boys sat tensely staring at the workstation, only their eyes moving. After a few minutes, the message "ACCESS SECURED" popped onto the screen. Kent twirled around in his chair and slapped Gene a high-five.

Once the program established access on another machine, certain security concerns were checked, and then if it appeared their access had not been detected, a copy of the program got uploaded to the new machine and run there to establish access to even more computers. By this means, the network of subservient computers grew at an exponential rate. Each machine monitored the machines it had accessed to ensure that Kent's unauthorized access would not be discovered. Status information was then passed back to the UW computer that Kent used.

After a while, the initial excitement faded, and the boys became tired. Gene went home, while Kent crawled into an old, yellow vinyl armchair and shut his eyes. He wanted to stay close to the computer in case it beeped out a warning of a security problem. He shifted uneasily at first from the discomfort of trying to sleep in the chair. Thoughts raced through his mind about the possibilities created by his handiwork, and jumbled together as he drifted off to sleep.

A nasal-sounding beep emerged from the computer with a rhythmic pulse. Kent snapped to attention and flung himself out of the chair at the workstation. The message "POSSIBLE DETECTION BY 137.243.2.31 — CODE 4, 03:27a" flashed on the screen. Kent's program had encountered a system with particularly good security, and apparently that computer had alerted its system operator.

Kent hit the side of the monitor. "Come on you piece of shit! Do something!"

"ATTEMPTING TO WRITE TO LOG FILE..." A few more seconds passed, but it seemed unbearably long to Kent.

"LOG FILE SUCCESSFULLY ALTERED, CONNECTION TERMINATED," the computer reported as it covered its tracks and withdrew.

Kent let out a sigh. He slowly looked up to see the workstation proceeding to access more computers, uncomprehending of what had just occurred. More than an hour had passed since he'd fallen asleep, but it had seemed like minutes. He settled down to sleep once more.

Kent got awakened sometime later by a similar beeping noise, but this time he had more confidence in his program's ability to take appropriate evasive actions, so he remained seated and watched the screen.

When the danger passed, Kent turned to the right and gazed out the fourth-story window. The sky had started to lighten, and a faint salmon color rimmed the eastern horizon. Some grayish clouds, their underside speckled a blood-red, hung farther up in the sky. Sleepiness again overtook Kent, and he slumped back in the chair.

Awakened a third time by a beeping noise, it turned out to be the alarm on his digital watch: 8:30 a.m. Some risk existed that an early-bird professor or eager student would come by.

Kent moved his head from side-to-side to loosen up his neck before walking over to the computer. He instructed his program to run in the "background" and to cease reporting its activities.

He went home and connected with the university computer with his PC to keep an eye on the program's progress. His father usually left him alone on Saturday mornings, while he went jogging, ate breakfast, and read his paper. John Dalton would then shower and head over to campus to catch up on his mail and stacks of reading material. This Saturday was no exception. Kent turned on his PC and crawled into bed before John returned from jogging.

As John entered the house covered with sweat, he noticed Kent's shoes by the kitchen door and realized Kent was home. He thought it strange that Kent would return from Gene's anytime before 10:30 in the morning, but he shrugged his shoulders as he walked to the refrigerator to get a glass of cranberry juice.

Kent awoke several hours later. He looked up at the ceiling where a fly crawled about upside down. He watched it for a minute or two wondering how it maintained its grip on the ceiling. He then reached over to his bedside stand and grabbed a plastic dart gun of sorts with a circular flyswatter projectile. He carefully took aim. "Make my day," he challenged. Fwop! Down came the fly and flyswatter, almost landing on Kent's head. He picked up the fly and held it a few inches from his face, studying it intently as it twitched with its last bit of life.

"Ah . . . fresh food for Spike." Kent got up, carried the fly over to his terrarium and fed it to his pet lizard.

Over the course of the week, the list of computer systems subject to Kent's control grew tremendously. By the time the weekend rolled around, Kent was ready to test the system. One of the best tests of computing power that he knew involved breaking encryption schemes. He knew a student in France had broken a 40-bit encryption scheme using 120 computer workstations and two supercomputers. It took the French student eight days to break the code. In a separate experiment, a German broke an RSA Data Security RC5 encrypted message in just 13 days using 5,000 volunteers connected via the Internet, each working on a fractional part of the problem when their computers were otherwise idle.

Kent was convinced he could do it more quickly. He already had assembled an arsenal of more than 6,100 computer systems with full-time access to the Net and could draw on a large but fluctuating number of PC's that may go online and offline sporadically. Kent also had the ability to draw on each full-time access machine on an around-the-clock basis through an automated process, not being hampered by waiting for volunteers to download chunks of the problem in their spare time. In addition, he had studied the algorithms employed in France and Germany and articles that analyzed them, and had devised what he believed was a more efficient code-breaking scheme.

Late Friday evening, Kent stopped over at Gene's house. "Hey Gene, let's ride over to campus and test MIPHSCI."

"Is it ready?"

"Yeah, I already debugged it by testing it on a much shorter encryption key."

The pair got on their bikes and rode toward campus. Kent looked over at his friend and smiled. "If only this wasn't illegal, I think we'd have some headline material. We've got the first practical, large-scale metacomputing system."

"Metacomputing?"

"Yeah, using multiple machines to handle parts of a computing task. It's like having an enormous parallel-processor supercomputer, except faster. Some universities have been trying to do something like this using Java programs distributed over the Web, but since Java programs are denied access to write on the disk of the machine they're running on, it's hard to do real work. Our system doesn't have that limitation."

The boys arrived at Sewart Hall, and Gene supplied an encrypted message for Kent to crack. Kent sat down at the computer workstation and fired up his network of computers and entered the message to be cracked.

After watching the program run for a few minutes, Kent got up from the chair. "Let's go get some pizza, and we'll check on this in a couple hours." Just as Gene put his hand on the doorknob, the computer beeped.

"Damn!" Kent exclaimed.

"I thought you said you debugged that thing."

They walked over to the workstation, and there on the screen was the encrypted message now in plain text, the code having been broken. Their jaws dropped.

"Holy Toledo!" Kent said.

"I don't believe it. Kent, you're a genius."

The two turned again to the computer and stared for a moment. Then they sat down and tested the program with more difficult encryption keys.

By the middle of the next week, Kent had thoroughly tested his encryption-smashing program, and he wanted to tell the world. However, since he used illegal means to accomplish this feat, he couldn't run to the local TV station with the news. Rather, he sent an e-mail message through an anonymous remailer computer in Finland to post a challenge to a cryptography newsgroup on the Internet. Under the on-line alias "Encryptomash" he boasted that he could crack any message encrypted with a 612-bit or smaller key within 48 hours.

Most of the people who read Kent's message just laughed, thinking such a feat impossible. A few decided to post encrypted messages anyway. Most of the encrypted messages were vulgar, mocking taunts directed at a person they did not believe could read them anyway.

One message stood out from the rest. The whole message was encrypted using the Pretty Good Privacy (PGP) public key Kent had posted with his challenge and was itself routed through an anonymous remailer, preventing Kent from knowing its origins. The use of Kent's public key allowed the sender to send a message Kent would be guaranteed to be able to read, but no one else. Kent used his copy of PGP to decrypt the message. It had two parts: a plain-text introduction followed by another encrypted message, this one with an unknown key. The plain-text portion was in poor English. It promised that "we give reward money for breaking other messages if can you break enclosed message."

Kent immediately set about breaking the encryption scheme. The following two nights he slept little. By the second morning, the message had been revealed. It read, "Congratulations! Please reply for further instructions." This one-line message was followed by a public encryption key for sending the reply so as to prevent others from reading it. In this way, Kent and the other unidentified person could send messages back and forth by posting them on the Internet where everyone could see them but no one could read them.

Kent added the public encryption key to his PGP software "key ring." It bore the name "Nick."

Kent posted a message on the newsgroup with evidence in plain text that he had indeed cracked the encryption scheme within 48 hours. This message was followed by encrypted text directed to Nick. In it Kent asked what he needed to do to get a reward.

Once Kent had proven that a 612-key encryption scheme could be breached in less than two days, the traffic on that newsgroup swelled ten-fold. Within a day, reports started to appear in the regular mass media that a hacker had succeeded in penetrating some of the best encryption available.

CHAPTER THIRTEEN

Moscow

Two quick knocks sounded from the door, followed by Kirill Kardirov's head peeking in, the *mafiya* lieutenant's face looking apologetic. "Excuse me for interrupting, but I have some potentially good news for you."

Nikolai Mikhailovich Volkov sat at the left end of his leather sofa with his right arm around a young, blonde woman. He did not look up from the big-screen TV on which he watched the movie *Fast & Furious* on DVD, but he did knock the volume down a few notches with the remote control. Peter the Great stared at the three from the label on a bottle of Pyotr Veliki vodka nesting in a chrome-plated bucket of ice on the glass coffee table. Volkov took a deep drag from the Marlboro in his left hand and slowly exhaled. "I hope you are going to tell me you have learned the details of when and where our government will be transporting the nuclear materiel. As you know, Kirill Ivanovich, our time is running out if we have any hope of intercepting it. To say the least, bonuses will be smaller this year if we lose out on several billion in hard currency."

"We do not have complete information yet, but we may have something better: a tool to get information about the nuclear transfer and much more."

"And what is this tool?"

"We have had contact over the Internet with a computer programmer who can break strong public key encryption such as that used by the government in many of its communications. No one in the world until now has been able to accomplish this."

"How do you know it is not the CIA or NSA?"

"We are confident for several reasons. First, our contacts tell us the messages from the programmer did not originate from the government. Second, the communications seem amateurish and juvenile. We think the work has been done by what the Americans call a 'hacker.'"

"How do you propose we acquire this technology?"

"We can offer money to buy it, of course. Since this person is capable of decoding secure messages, we can encode our offer so nobody else knows the transaction is taking place. That also minimizes the chance that we will be stuck in competitive bidding, at least if we move quickly. And if we cannot buy the technology, we will just take it."

"Very good. Proceed." Volkov turned the volume up just in time for an explosion to rumble from the Surround Sound speakers, shaking the apartment.

Madison

The following day, Kent found an encrypted message from Nick instructing him to check for a message posted on a different, less busy newsgroup where they were less likely to draw attention to themselves. The second message offered Kent $100,000 cash in exchange for his encryption-breaking program. Kent was flabbergasted, having never earned more than $8.00 per hour at any job. He had to turn down the offer because his encryption breaking scheme partially involved a hardware solution, the illegal network of computers, not susceptible to being sold.

Kent struggled with how to respond. He was certainly willing to take money for the use of his program, but how much could he get for cracking one message at a time as opposed to selling his methodology? He did not know whether Nick was serious and had the money to back up his offer. He briefly considered demanding $50,000. He might even be able to demand $75,000. Suspecting that he would not get such large amounts, he wrote back and offered to crack messages for Nick for $15,000 for the first message and $10,000 for subsequent messages, reasonable sums he figured, if the encrypted messages were significant enough. He dreamed of handling a volume of work that could quickly add up in a few weeks to well over $100,000.

In the meantime, individuals, universities, and government officials posted messages asking "Encryptomash" to reveal his secret, some offering money and others offering to publish his work. Yet others offered employment. Kent knew he had to play his cards carefully lest someone discover that he was cheating.

He could not resist responding to a couple more of the messages. Invariably, each curious person posted their own encrypted message as a test of Encryptomash's skills. Kent solved a couple such puzzles and posted the results.

He began to doubt more and more each day that Nick or his money would ever materialize. "Too good to be true," Kent feared.

CHAPTER FOURTEEN

Kent picked at the corner of his thumbnail. "I'd kinda like to get closer to Sam. I feel like I'm making some progress with her, but I can never really read her feelings."

"When I've seen you two together," Gene answered, "she seemed pretty upbeat."

"But it's always me who suggests we do things, and even then she usually says no. When I suggested we get together on Friday or Saturday, she said she already had plans with friends."

"You might be reading too much into it."

"Maybe. All I know for sure is how great it feels to be with her. I'm going to marry that girl. It's only a matter of time."

Gene chuckled.

"No, I mean it. It may sound corny, but I believe it's destiny."

"It seems a little early to tell. Just last week you told me that you brought pizza and beer with you for the tutoring session, but it was like being out with a sister or first cousin."

"There just weren't any sparks. I felt like I did all the talking. It's hard to explain."

CIA Headquarters, Langley, Virginia

"Jensen, what the hell is going on down there with your operation in Quibdo?" asked Vernon Coles, chief of the Latin American Division of the Operations Directorate of the CIA. Coles was a nondescript man, his hair thinning and gray. He paced during most of these weekly briefings. If he sat down at all, it was only to scribble a couple notes before he bounced up and started to carve away on another subordinate in his division.

People who worked for him either quickly learned to tolerate the intense demands and frequent criticism, or moved on to a different division or out of the Central Intelligence Agency altogether. Some agents enjoyed sparring with Coles. Others adopted a stoic approach. They all realized more serious challenges faced them than Coles' demeanor.

"Well, in addition to dealing with the private armies of the drug lords around that Colombian city, a new element has been introduced: the Russian *mafiya* appears to have joined the fray," Jensen explained. "We're not sure what the scope of the *mafiya's* involvement is yet, but they seem to be supplying arms in exchange for cash. We suspect they're also working on the money-laundering end of things, and they're not afraid to use violence. Two of our agents have died, and several others have been wounded in the name of gathering intelligence to fight the war on drugs. The criminal element there is as well equipped with surveillance technology as we are, and they have us outgunned."

Coles stopped pacing, looked at Jensen, and grabbed the edge of the table to hold himself in place. When he spoke again, the people sitting across the table had to strain to hear him. "Damn it." Blood vessels bulged in his neck as he strained to contain himself. "We're blowing our budget, our people are getting killed, and we're not accomplishing anything. I want you to smoke those bastards out, and I mean that literally. Let them get a strong whiff of their own burning coca fields. I'll make sure you have the people, the guns and the napalm to do the job right."

The agents sitting around the table were shocked by the implications of what their boss had ordered. While everyone empathized with the difficulties the operatives inside Colombia were facing, a line existed that even the CIA was not supposed to cross, and with a presidential commission scrutinizing their activities, even greater caution was required. Coles had essentially ordered a small scale, covert war as opposed to merely defensive actions, and such operations always seemed to grow on their own beyond the original plans.

The meeting topic switched to Encryptomash and his ability to pry open what were thought to be secure communications. It was not the direct responsibility of this group of operatives to gather intelligence about Encryptomash, particularly since he was not thought to be in Latin America, but the importance of the technology created a competitive spirit. Everyone in the intelligence community wanted to be the first to locate Encryptomash and acquire his technology.

After the meeting, the participants cleared out like water droplets evaporating on a hot griddle. Coles stayed behind to look over some of the written briefings he had received. When he wanted to get some reading done, he found it easier away from the distractions of his desk and phone.

Agent Paul Burrell popped his head back in the conference room. Burrell was a tall, black man with chiseled features and an athletic frame. His work in the field had included posing as a resident of various tropical islands in the Caribbean as he tracked the flow of money in and out of offshore banks from illegal operations.

He wore a worried look on his face. He stood in the doorway without making a noise, and Coles did not notice him. He took a step into the room and shuffled his feet to alert Coles of his presence.

Coles glanced over his shoulder before returning his gaze to the papers on the table. "Burrell. I thought you had a meeting across the Potomac."

"I do. I just wanted to touch base with you about today's discussion."

"What about it?"

Burrell shifted his weight from one foot to the other. "Well, I get the feeling we were all a little surprised by what you told Jensen to do." Burrell swallowed. "To be perfectly frank, if you're serious, I think you've gone mad."

Coles answered carefully, "Look, I'm not totally insensitive to your concerns, but you've been around and seen this shit. You know what's going on down there. I've got all those people in the field whose spouses and kids are depending on me to get them back in one piece. I'm frigging sick and tired of kissing politicians' asses every damn day to try to keep them off my back, while at the same time my people are putting it all on the line. And for what? Someone's got to do something."

"I understand what you're saying, but I question your methods on this one."

Madison

Kent had determined to make the evening of tutoring a bit more interesting, and again ran through the list of campus activities and community events. He thought about asking her out to dinner, a play, a museum, but finally decided that a movie represented the way to go. He could make it seem spontaneous, not like he was asking for a date. It also might provide the opportunity for Kent to put his arm around her in a dark room, and if it went well, perhaps he could even coax her into resting her head on his shoulder—small steps he realized, but moving in the right direction. He didn't intend to risk scaring her off by moving too fast.

On Tuesday evening, Kent arrived at Sam's dorm room ten minutes early.

"Well, I'm glad you're here," Sam said. "Our new programming assignment has me all confused."

Kent raced through Sam's assignment. He did most of the work, but usually took the time to explain each step. On this occasion he didn't wait for any acknowledgment of his brief explanation. A fast typist, his long, thin fingers cut, pasted, deleted and pounded out new code so quickly that Sam didn't have a chance to follow what he did.

Kent finished fixing the program in fifteen minutes. "Hey, since we're done early, why don't we catch a movie—I haven't been to one in a while," Kent said, as if the thought had just occurred to him.

It took Sam a moment to snap out of her mental wanderings and realize Kent had said something requiring a response. "Hmm, yeah, I suppose we could. I sure am sick of studying. You know, we could save a lot of time and learn this stuff faster if the professors gave us an outline of their lecture notes before class."

"What would you like to see?" Kent said, steering the conversation back to movies. Even after all his planning for the evening, Kent had neglected to check on what movie to suggest. He didn't know what kind of pictures she liked, and figured it would be different from what he liked to see: action movies, comedies and horror films. She probably went for dramas and romantic stories. Blech! Of course, if it took a romantic movie to get her in the mood, Kent figured he could tolerate it.

"What's playing?" she asked.

Kent felt like smacking himself in the head. "I don't know. Do you have a campus paper?"

"Helen, do you have one?" Sam asked.

Helen looked up from her book pretending not to have heard the conversation. "One what?"

"A campus newspaper. We want to check the movie listings."

"Just a second." Helen finished the paragraph she was reading, then fumbled for a bookmark she'd misplaced on the rumpled bedspread. She rolled off the bed and dug through a stack of magazines and loose pieces of paper. She located the newspaper and handed it to Sam.

The pages snapped as Sam flipped the paper open. She studied the listings. "Why not this Tom Cruise flick? It's been out a while, but I haven't seen it."

Kent smiled with genuine pleasure. "Yeah, that would be great." Her only interest probably involved seeing Tom Cruise, but Kent looked forward to seeing this action film anyway.

"The movie doesn't start for twenty-five minutes," Sam said, "but it will take us about ten minutes to walk there. We might as well head out now."

An awkward silence enveloped them as they walked down the sidewalk. The silence suffocated Kent as if he held his breath underwater. During the tutoring sessions he'd avoided this feeling by talking about the computer programs they worked on. Now nothing filled the void. Kent studied the texture of the newly-laid concrete under their feet.

"That computer program tonight was a breeze," Kent said to break the silence. As soon as the words came out, he wished he could take them back. Sam told him the program had her confused, and now he'd told her it's a breeze, as if to mock her. "I mean, once you get the algorithm down, the rest just kind of falls into place."

"Hmm," Sam replied.

Kent thought about how much he would like to hold Sam's hand, but figured that would seem too juvenile: worse, it would expose him to possible rejection.

Sam broke the awkward silence with an old fallback: the weather. "Brrr, it's really cold tonight. Just two days ago it was pleasant, and all of a sudden this."

"Yeah, that's Wisconsin. Nine months of winter and three months of road construction."

Sam half chuckled, and the smile lingered on her face. Kent couldn't help but stare at her beautiful features and study the lines of her face.

Sam felt his stare and turned her head and looked him in the eyes with a puzzled but happy expression on her face.

Kent shyly turned away to look ahead. "What's your favorite Tom Cruise movie?" he asked.

"Oh, I don't know. It's hard to say. I really liked that one with Nicole Kidman where they played Irish immigrants—I can't remember the name.

"*Far and Away.*"

"Yeah. I also liked *Top Gun.*"

"Me too! A great movie. That was cool when they were flying inverted over the MiG fighter."

"Yeah, but I really like the part near the end when he's sitting in the diner and the jukebox starts playing 'You Lost that Lovin' Feeling.'"

Kent thought for a moment. He had seen plenty of movies, but he couldn't remember any more with Tom Cruise. "Oh, how 'bout *Cocktail?*" he asked when that came to mind.

"I don't think I saw it. What's it about?"

"Uh, Tom plays a business school student. Starts bartending. Goes to some tropical island, falls in love, gets his girlfriend pregnant, screws up the relationship. He didn't know she was pregnant, but he meets up with her later in New York. Tom ends up marrying the girl and they live happily ever after. It ends with Tom in his own, new bar—Cocktails & Dreams—standing on the bar telling grand poems about his soon to be expanding family with his very pregnant wife, and then he finds out she's about to have twins."

"Hmm."

Not a very impressive rendition, Kent thought. "It was an okay movie."

The two turned a corner, and the theater slid into view. Fingers of light from the old marquee darted out and grasped around the shiny contours of a black Celica parked along the curb between them and the theater. A fair number of people waited on the sidewalk to get in. Kent and Sam joined the throng.

A pair of teenage boys with longish hair slid in front of them. "Jerks," Sam snapped, loud enough for them to hear.

Kent winced and looked away. He didn't like confronting people, and didn't want a scene to develop. The boys in front ignored Sam.

Kent and Sam reached the ticket booth. "Two adults," Kent said, sliding the money through the hole in the glass. The bored cashier slid two tickets out to him. "Thanks," Kent said. The cashier did not reply.

"Boy, there are a lot of rude people around tonight," he said as he walked by the candy counter. "Would you like anything?"

"Diet cola—medium. What are you going to have?"

"I'm not really thirsty."

After Kent bought the soda, they strolled in and sat down in one of the few areas with empty seats. No music played, and the sound of a hundred simultaneous conversations buzzed about them.

It seemed to Kent he must be the only person in the theater without anything to say. He checked his watch—10 minutes to show time. There were so many things he wanted to share with Sam, to talk to her about, but his mind had run way ahead of the stage they were in to things like marriage, children, and careers. He figured mentioning any of those would send Sam running out of the theater.

Kent found it difficult to concentrate. Usually he immersed himself into the events unfolding on the screen, but tonight he was nagged by thoughts of how to act around Sam and how to advance the relationship. By the middle of the movie, he resolved to put his arm around her. After much hesitation and second-guessing, he reached around behind her with his right arm but kept his hand off her right shoulder. His arm rested more on the back of her chair than on her shoulders. He was glad when she didn't react. Even if she did mind, she wasn't expressing it and Kent could live with that. He smiled and turned his thoughts back to the movie.

Kent's right arm began to ache. He debated with himself whether to move it. He decided against, because he imagined Sam would think him a wimp, or that for some other reason he didn't want to hold her anymore.

By the end of the movie, Kent's arm had fallen asleep from

the shoulder down. It didn't matter, because from Sam's comments about the movie, he could tell she had enjoyed it. At least one of them had been able to concentrate.

A cold wind slapped their faces as they stepped through the doors. Sam shuddered and jammed her hands into her pockets. "Well, I need to get back and get some sleep. I've got a quiz in my marketing class tomorrow."

Kent folded his arms and drew them tightly against himself. "I'll walk you home."

"No, you don't have to. That's quite a bit out of the way for you."

Kent didn't know whether to interpret that as an attempt to get rid of him or an effort to be considerate. "I'm going that way anyway. My bike is at your dorm."

"Oh, okay."

They walked a half block in silence until Kent spoke up. "Cool stunts in the movie, don't ya think?"

"Yeah, it had me hanging on the edge of my seat."

"I especially like explosions and pyrotechnics. I do a little of that myself."

Sam turned to him, eyes wide and mouth open. "You do what?"

"Yeah, everything from homemade Roman candles to plastic explosives."

Sam's eyes narrowed with skepticism. "You're kidding."

Kent shook his head. "No, why would I be kidding?"

"I guess I could see making Roman candles, but why mess with plastic explosives?"

"I don't know. It's fun."

"It's dangerous."

"I'm pretty careful."

"I still don't know why you'd want to do that."

"It's a challenge. It's a lot like hacking computers. It's forbidden, and it's the ultimate test of one's knowledge and abilities—gathering guarded information and applying it to do things that most people can't or won't do."

"I hope you don't go around blowing up buildings."

Kent playfully pushed on Sam's shoulder. "Hey! I'm not a nut. I just like to have a little fun."

"I'm sorry. It sounds a little crazy."

"Well, to paraphrase Thoreau, I wish to live deliberately, and not, when I come to die, discover that I had not lived. I want to live deep and suck out all the marrow of life."

Sam giggled. "You might be living deep alright—six feet under."

The next day at high school, Kent eagerly told Gene about the night's events. As eager to listen as Kent was to describe what happened, Gene had largely resigned himself to living vicariously through the romantic and/or sexual exploits of others. He had convinced himself he would never find anyone attracted to him.

CHAPTER FIFTEEN

After Kent responded to Nick's e-mail offer, a message bearing Nick's PGP signature was posted: "Your demand is unreasonable. I will not be able to tell how valuable your service is until after message is deciphered. Will pay $2,000 for individual message."

Kent initially read the message with happy surprise, which quickly turned to cynicism. "I'm never going to see a dime from this," he thought. He wrote back, "I need $8,000 per message. Pay half down and the balance on successful completion."

Within twelve hours he received a response from Nick agreeing to these terms and asking how payment should be handled. Kent quickly went about opening an account at a bank whose computer system he already had access to. He used a fake ID so he could establish an account without his father's signature. He then replied with the name of the bank and the account number so money could be wire-transferred. Kent figured he might be in a better position to monitor the transactions due to his access to that bank's computer.

Early the next morning, Kent connected with the university computer and checked his e-mail from home. The first message to crack waited there along with a note that a $4,000 down payment had been deposited in his account. Kent first checked the bank account and confirmed the presence of the money, which he immediately transferred to his regular savings account at a different bank.

Next, he called Gene's house on the phone. "Gene, I got four thousand bucks! It's for real!"

"No way."

"Yes, way. I'll give you a cut tomorrow. . . unless you don't want it."

"Of course I want it. Are you sure you're not kidding me?"

"I'm sure. I'll start decoding the message right away so we can make even more money. We're gonna be rich!"

"Yeah, well how rich am I gonna be compared to you? How big a cut were you thinking of giving me?"

"I don't know. I hadn't really thought about it," Kent lied. "How about twenty-five percent?"

Gene thought it over for a moment. "I s'pose that would be okay." Gene had thought Kent would offer only ten percent, but he didn't want Kent believing he had received too good of a deal. "What do you think the message is anyway? Why would someone pay that much money to someone they don't even know?"

"They must need the information bad."

"Yeah, I'd say. *I* wouldn't trust you with all that money."

"Well, you're gonna have to to get your share. I'll see ya at school."

Kent set his program in motion to decode the message, then went downstairs for a quick breakfast before school.

"What's got you in such a good mood?" John inquired of his son.

"I don't know. It just seems like a nice day."

"Yes, it is," John said, thinking it was always a nice day when he didn't have a teenager complaining about chores or students with their petty disagreements over whether something was "cool" or not.

Over the course of the next couple days, Kent checked on the progress of his program several times. He had written the program to allow information to be displayed on its progress at any point. It was particularly important to be able to monitor its progress, since the program relied on the resources of thousands of individual computer systems whose response times could be highly variable due to maintenance shut-downs and other demands on each system.

It seemed to take an unusually large amount of time to decode the message from Nick, and Kent didn't know why. Unfortunately, he had no way to tell in advance the size of the "key" used to encrypt the message, and possibly the author had used a larger key than Kent expected. Without knowing the size of the key, Kent could get little useful information from the program regarding how long it would take to complete its task.

After two days, Kent received a message from Nick inquiring about his progress. "It's still working—I'm sure we'll crack it very soon," Kent replied. Despite the optimistic tone of his response, Kent had gotten worried. What would happen if he didn't come through? he wondered.

Kent ran into Gene in the hallway at high school. "Well?" Gene inquired.

"Nothing yet."

"Nick is going to think you stole his money."

"No, he won't. He knows we'll make twice as much if we complete the job." But Kent couldn't be sure Nick would be so understanding.

Kent checked again several times on the third day. The program continued crunching numbers. By 4:00 p.m., Kent knew something was wrong. He went home, dropped on the bed, and lay motionless.

Finally he got up and stepped over to the PC on his desk. It was already on: Kent rarely shut it off. Usually some program was running, churning away in his absence. Kent connected with his university account. The program was done! Kent entered the command to display the results. The computer prompted Kent for a password, he typed it in, and the screen filled with the characters comprising the message:

Y9sXBv pulXy/oJ0. kcD eQiGJ
RIKLyoaV3eM J7E/sRu3s lWYNBZ k2
XwfOnqY FBEG rOxT0Yi JUhg9
VzYeRZ7NB 0WOW9qAo c X/Uo3J.
1u/eSyO0S 7jH Q68KMbv+x 2a K9PAAU
RtC JEYXZpZCBBIE hpr NNjaCA
8ZGF2 aW RAaW93Ywxhd y5jb20+iQ L
VAwUQL0efk. KMbv +x2aK9PA AMO
8wP9EhtkRD J t76OK9Y
gZw0LOJU25UJIsk5 L +zNkwWk7vdo JcJ
9E/HK4JL Wdq10x. AOwJcxXTl+O
H+rytz ZLJfD UqC dMa4ZV7MYoF+
kB2Nve 56f7v/TrjF Ef kPar/aX YfUh9
mSEG2+X5 E9I wdJCG 4lsgYoZh. XsXz
crg/v1 ZRNcD HfUTlE=Q59G.

"What!" Kent exclaimed out loud. "That can't be." The screen was filled with gibberish. There did appear to be some order to the characters: the letters were grouped into word-like units separated by spaces but remained totally unintelligible. "It must be another level of encryption," he said to himself. He printed the results nevertheless. He never trusted computers to be the sole storage medium for anything that took considerable time to produce. Too often he had experienced disks crashing and data loss. Hard copy was the best protection against that.

He called Gene's house and skipped the pleasantries when Gene answered the phone. "You won't believe it."

"What?"

"It's done, but it's not done. It's just gibberish. There must be another level of encryption. Why don't you come over and help me."

"I'm gonna eat soon."

Kent sighed. "Hurry up. This is important."

Kent struggled with the problem, pouring over books he had on encryption to determine what method had been used.

Gene showed up 45 minutes later. The two spent the whole evening trying to crack the code. None of the programs they used did the trick.

"Damn, I just don't know what to do," Kent said.

"What are we gonna tell Nick?"

"Maybe we can put him off for a couple more days."

"I don't think that's a good idea. His last message didn't sound too friendly."

"He can't possibly know where we are, anyway. What's he gonna do about it?"

"How can you be sure he doesn't know where we are? People who wire transfer thousands of dollars around to people they've never met must have connections."

"Maybe we should just send him the results. He might know what type of additional encryption they're using. We did the hard part already, at least the part that's hard in theory."

"If we tell him, he might get really pissed off."

"No, if we're honest with him, he'll be less anxious about it. We'll give him what we have and tell him we're hard at work to finish the job."

"Well, that might work."

"It'll have to." Kent immediately set about drafting e-mail to inform Nick of the status of their work, and he included an apology. He attached the computer file of nonsensical characters to demonstrate his efforts to crack the code.

CHAPTER SIXTEEN

Berlin

The sign with red Arabic letters leaped out from its drab surroundings. *Mafiya* boss Nikolai Volkov and his beefy bodyguard approached the store, scanning the urban terrain from behind dark sunglasses. They paused a moment at the entrance and looked once more before ducking inside. Traditional Middle-Eastern music greeted them as the closed door sealed out the noises of the street. Although the storefront was mostly glass, a partition wall had been set back a short distance, ostensibly to display additional merchandise. The store housed antiques mixed with contemporary items.

Volkov and his companion walked about the front area, examining separate pieces. After a moment, they walked farther back, stepping past the partition. A clerk approached, greeted them in German, and asked whether he could help. "No, I'm just looking," Volkov replied.

Several minutes passed while the Russians studied antiques. Then Volkov approached the clerk and asked to see an astrolabe.

"I am sorry. We are all out at the moment. I do expect some to arrive soon. Please look around while you wait."

While the clerk walked over to the phone, Volkov picked up an old, leather-bound book and leafed through the pages. Ten minutes passed. Volkov said to his bodyguard, "They are slower than Russian bureaucrats."

Four bearded men, members of the Iranian intelligence service Etallat, entered from the back door. One with thick eyebrows spanning the bridge of his nose walked straight to the front of the store, while two others studied Volkov and his bodyguard. The oldest one approached the clerk. Whispers were exchanged in Farsi, and they glanced at Volkov. The oldest one smiled at last, walked over to Volkov and introduced himself as Ahmad. The two Russians were ushered into a back room with three of the Iranians; the fourth remained by the front entrance as a sentinel.

"Gentlemen," Volkov said, "we will soon be able to provide you with significant quantities of plutonium—enough to transform the politics of your corner of the world and beyond."

"We are not convinced that you will be able to honor your promises," Ahmad said. "What happens when we make the inevitable down payment and you don't deliver the goods?"

"I am disappointed you do not have more confidence in us. Has Fazullah not given us a better recom-mendation than that?" Volkov said, referring to the Iranian contact for the prior sale of nuclear materials.

"Fazullah said good things about the quality of the uranium, but he hoped for larger quantities."

"As I'm sure he explained, we are not a small operation, and we are backed by significant experience. Our network includes former officers of the Russian Army, former high-ranking KGB members, and a solid group of nuclear, computer and financial experts."

"We are concerned that you have not taken on an operation of this size previously."

"With all respect, that is where you are mistaken. Our organization has handled several jobs of comparable scale and difficulty, and the best part is we have worked so discretely and effectively that when governments do discover problems, they're too embarrassed to reveal anything to the public. Furthermore, our people have been involved in much larger operations while in their previous official capacities."

"How is it you intend to gain possession of the nuclear materials?"

"Our primary plan is to intercept them while in transit by rail."

Ahmad thought for a moment. "We don't want to take chances. We will provide a training base so your people can work out any potential difficulties. There will be only one opportunity to accomplish this."

Volkov and his bodyguard returned to their hotel, and Volkov found a phone message waiting for him from Kirill Kardirov. Kardirov had not left a name, merely instructing the front desk to tell Volkov to "call home."

Volkov locked his hotel room door and performed a quick sweep for listening devices. He connected a voice scrambler to the phone, and called Kardirov on a line they reserved for secure communications.

Kardirov answered.

"You called?" Volkov responded.

"Yes, I wanted to keep you updated. We received the first message. The Ministry has completed its inventory at one location and is awaiting instructions for shipment. It won't be ready to go for at least two weeks."

"That is good news. Our small investment in encryption technology is paying off."

"I have other good news. As we anticipated, Encryptomash cannot read what he has decoded. He sent the message to us with an apology. He thinks there is another level of encryption."

"For him, there is. Send him the next one. Let him keep the $4,000 for his efforts, but cut payment in half for future messages to keep him from being suspicious."

"I will."

"Have you made any progress in locating him?"

"No, it is extremely difficult. We have people working on it."

"Any other developments I should be aware of?"

"Just that we received a large amount of cash from Brighton Beach."

"Good. My negotiations here have been productive, and I will return to Moscow tomorrow. I want to discuss our New York money laundering operations then."

Volkov ended the call and settled into a plush sofa with a stack of financial reports from his operations. He insisted on reviewing these himself despite having the best accountants money could buy.

A while later, he heard a pounding on the door. "Nikolasha, open up!" said Aleksandra, his female companion, using an endearing form of his name.

Volkov looked through the peephole in the door, unlocked it and let her in. She carried a couple large department store bags.

Aleksandra's flowing, raven black hair reflected highlights from her new, crimson dress that paralleled the color of her glossy lips. Volkov peered into her eyes, glowing pools of amber brown. He noticed unfamiliar pearl earrings and a gold rope chain necklace suspending a solitary pearl. His gaze dropped to her stretch ottoman knit dress with a low, square neckline held up by spaghetti straps. The fabric tightly hugged her ample breasts, and the short hem exposed most of her slender legs. Even her anklewrap snakeskin pumps were new.

"I hope you didn't have any trouble finding where to shop," Volkov said.

Aleksandra smiled and swung a shopping bag past Volkov's shoulder. "Oh, knock it off. They had such fabulous stuff," she said, setting her bags on a table. "You've got to take me to Berlin more often."

Volkov rubbed his forehead. "You would run me broke." He walked across the room and poured himself a drink. "What would you like to do this evening?"

"You need to ask? I've been dying to see some of the nightclubs here."

"Okay, as long as you promise not to shop for the rest of the trip."

"Actually, I had something better in mind than shopping right now. That Jacuzzi looks inviting."

Aleksandra closed in on Volkov and began kissing his neck while she ran her hand down his back and pulled him tightly against her. Using her other hand, she slowly unbuttoned his shirt and ran her fingers through his chest hair. She looked into his dark, yearning eyes and pressed her lips against his. After a long, hungry kiss, she stepped back, knocked the straps of her dress off her shoulders, and tugged the dress down to the floor. After she finished undressing him, they stumbled over to the Jacuzzi, lips and arms still interlocked, and eased into the steamy froth.

Northampton, Massachusetts

Samantha Trzebiatowski woke up but kept her eyes closed, inhaling deeply through her nose. She loved the smell of fresh sheets on her bed at home. She thought about the beautiful weather on the flight home the day before, the colorful trees and golden grasslands under a cool, blue sky.

She would be home again in a few weeks for Thanksgiving, but hadn't wanted to wait that long. Her parents were glad to see her and happy to pay for the plane tickets whenever she traveled to Massachusetts. Sam flew despite having a Saab to drive. The car only went between Madison and home at the beginning and end of the school year.

She opened her eyes without lifting her head from the pillow. It was just after nine o'clock. She could be out shopping with her mother by eleven.

She glanced up from her bedside stand to a shelf on the wall that held trophies and awards from her high school days. She was most proud of her riding trophies—she loved horses and had spent much time with them in shows. In college, her infrequent trips to Massachusetts afforded few opportunities to ride during the school year, but summers back home were filled with riding. She had hoped to meet a Wisconsin resident at the university who owned horses to give her more time in the saddle.

Sam slipped out of bed and went to her window. Her dad stood outside across the expansive back yard cleaning up the remains of the small vegetable garden. She'd expected him to be at his company, or on the golf course.

Sam showered, dressed, and walked down the oak staircase to the kitchen where her mother busied herself arranging flowers in a vase.

"Good morning, Samantha," Betty Trzebiatowski said with a big smile.

"Morning, Mom." Hearing her full, first name almost sounded foreign now. She'd become accustomed to being called "Sam" at college.

"You're just in time. I made your favorite—a Belgian waffle. I started it when I heard you leave the shower."

"Thanks. It's not often I get a good breakfast like this."

"How are your classes going, sweetie?"

Sam took a bite of her waffle. "Good. I was having some trouble with my computer class at the beginning of the semester, but I have a tutor now."

"Is your tutor a graduate student?"

"No," Sam chuckled. "Actually he's a high school senior. His name's Kent."

"High school?"

"Kent is basically a genius. He's seventeen or eighteen and still in high school, but he takes some college classes too."

"Speaking of boys. . ."

"Mom," Sam protested.

"I was just curious. You haven't really talked about anyone lately."

"There hasn't been anyone lately."

"I'm not trying to rush you. It would just be nice if you found a boy—someone you eventually could marry."

"It's not like I have trouble getting dates or anything. For that matter, I went to a movie with Kent. I think he might have considered it a date, but he's just not my type."

"Of course, I don't know anything about this Kent person, but it wouldn't hurt to date someone smart and stable. You know, your father wasn't exactly Cary Grant when I met him, but he was smart, hardworking, and a shrewd businessman, and it didn't take long before he ran the company."

Sam munched on her Belgian waffle and tried to ignore her mother's last comment.

CHAPTER SEVENTEEN

Madison

In response to Kent's status report and apology, he received a message from Nick sent by Kardirov the following morning:

> I received your message with the unreadable file attached. I will see what I can do to decode it. I will let you keep the $4,000 this time, but you must keep working to break more than the public key encryption. For future messages, payment will be cut in half unless fully decoded.

It surprised Kent that Nick's response had not been more negative. Nick must have confidence he could accomplish something useful, and therefore tried to maintain the relationship.

Kent was even more surprised to receive another encoded message from Nick a day and a half later with $2,000 deposited in his account. Kent called Gene to report the news.

"Wow," Gene said, "this guy is either a real sucker, or really desperate."

"I don't care what he is as long as he continues to pay, even if it is less money than before."

"We better get it right this time."

"I've already got the program running. We've been able to access about a thousand more computer systems, so the work should go faster this time."

Kent and Gene broke the first level of encryption more quickly with the second message from Nick, but still ended up with gibberish. With some misgivings, they sent the nonsensical characters on to Nick. About three hours later, a response showed up in Kent's computer "in-box" stating the second message had been received, but no progress had been made to make either one readable.

Kent had expected Nick's response, but it left him disappointed. How could Kent thwart one of the most powerful encryption schemes in the world, and yet be left with a senseless pile of characters? He knew a way existed to crack this mystery. Whatever encryption scheme used, it had weaknesses, as certain patterns emerged from the otherwise obscure text.

At first glance, it appeared to be a simple substitution of characters, but Kent tried that first, and could not crack it. He ran the messages through a program, checking the frequency with which characters occurred in the encrypted text, comparing that with normal occurrence rates for each letter of the alphabet. He came up empty-handed.

The author of these messages had sophistication, and the message content must be of great importance, Kent thought. He assumed he dealt either with big business or the military. With this in mind, Kent became more determined to crack the messages. "Why let Nick cash in on these secrets?" Kent thought. "Maybe I can cash in myself. If Nick is willing to pay me several thousands of dollars, there must be hundreds of thousands or millions at stake."

Kent knew some people on the Net who were real geniuses of encryption technology, and he considered passing on the messages for them to crack, but he resisted the temptation. If they could read the content of the messages, they might figure out a way to cut Kent out of the picture and cash in themselves. This could not be risked, at least as long as he continued to be paid something from Nick. If the funds dried up, then maybe he would consider seeking help.

The following week, while Kent sat at home during the evening reading the journal *Science*, he received a phone call from Sam asking to meet him the following day so she could give him a copy of her revised C.S. syllabus and have him check over a program she intended to hand in. They agreed to meet at the foreign languages lab where Sam would be working on her French homework.

The next day, Kent walked over to the languages center ten minutes ahead of schedule, pulling out a small bottle of cologne from his backpack as he walked. He dabbed some on a finger and smeared it on his neck. Since he'd begun tutoring Sam, he'd made a point of carrying cologne with him.

He walked into the building, found the right room, and saw Sam sitting by the windows with headphones on as she listened to a French language tape. He tapped her on the shoulder, and she spun around, startled.

"Oh, hi, Kent." She pulled the headphones off her ears while keeping them on her head. "Will you be able to wait a few minutes while I finish this tape? Then we can go over the program."

"No problem."

"It won't take much longer." Sam slipped the headphones back down.

Kent wandered around the language lab, looking at students with headphones and others typing away on computers in foreign languages. One computer screen in particular caught his attention, as it was filled with strange characters. Kent watched for a few minutes as the student, even scrawnier than he and wearing an outdated late-Seventies style of plastic-rimmed glasses, pecked away at the keys while looking at a cheat sheet showing which keys to press on the standard keyboard to get the foreign characters to appear on the screen.

"Kent."

He turned around to see Sam had finished with her tape. "Where do you want to go over your C.S. homework?"

"We can do it right over here," she replied, gesturing to a corner of the room with sufficient space for two. Kent looked over her program, and spent the next fifteen minutes scribbling computer code on a notepad.

When he finished the program, the two of them got up and started to walk out of the lab. The scrawny guy still plugged away at the keyboard, somewhat faster now. As Kent started to go past, the student reached for the mouse and clicked on the "page preview" icon at the top of the screen. The computer quickly drew the image of a page and filled it with characters to show the layout of the text. The image caught the corner of Kent's eye, and he turned to look directly at the computer monitor. In place of the foreign characters previously filling the screen, the page image contained small letters of the Roman alphabet, but it appeared to be gibberish. At that resolution, the computer had drawn the normal characters assigned to the keyboard, rather than the exotic typeface that had been displayed at full size.

"What the. . ." Kent leaned over the student's shoulder and squinted at the screen. "What language is that? Greek?"

The student turned around with a puzzled look. "No, it's Russian, but you can't see the Cyrillic letters now when I'm in page preview mode."

"Russian," Kent repeated. "How do you get Russian characters?"

"It's a Windows font just like any other."

Sam cleared her throat. "I'll see you later."

"Okay, just get me the disk," Kent said without looking at her. He turned to the male student. "Could I make a copy of your keyboard template?"

"Uh, sure. There's a copier in the next room. Costs a dime. Are you gonna be studying Russian?"

"Yeah, I think I will be."

After getting a copy of the template, Kent ran to the campus bookstore and bought a Russian-English dictionary. Next he sprinted to the engineering building and sat in front of a computer, skipping the college class he was supposed to attend.

He accessed his account and displayed the latest message he'd deciphered from Nick. He painstakingly rewrote the message, character by character, substituting Cyrillic letters for the Roman ones. He wasn't sure how to print letters from the Russian alphabet, and it took a full 40 minutes to rewrite the message. By the time he finished, he had to leave campus and return to high school. He was angry at not having a chance to translate what he had written, but it wouldn't be so easy to cut class at Emerson High.

Finally, lunchtime rolled around. He found Gene, carrying a plate heaped with food. "Gene, you won't believe what I figured out."

"What?"

"I think I found the secret to the encrypted messages. They're in Russian—the letters just have to be converted from Roman to Cyrillic and then we have to translate it."

"Yeah?"

"I picked up a Russian-English dictionary. I've already converted the characters into Russian, but I haven't started to translate it yet. As soon as we're done eating, we can start working on it."

In the library, Kent spent a few moments familiarizing himself with the Russian dictionary and the order of letters. By the time he started looking up the first word, Gene arrived. "Here, look at what we have," Kent instructed, sliding the paper across the small square table.

"Russian, huh. How did you figure that out?"

"I'll tell you later. I'll look up the words, and you write down the English translation."

"Okay."

Not knowing the first thing about the Russian alphabet, Kent went back and forth through the dictionary trying to find the first word.

"Can't you find it?"

"No, I don't see anything like it."

"Are you sure it's Russian?"

"I don't know."

"Well, maybe. . ."

"Hold it," Kent interrupted. "I was looking in the wrong spot. I think the first one is 'inventory.'"

"What the hell is this?" Kent mumbled in reference to the second word. A few more minutes passed. "Well, this one here must be 'complete.'"

Kent could not find several words even after going back and forth through the dictionary. He didn't know if such words were proper nouns or maybe just different forms of the words that didn't appear in the dictionary.

"What have we got so far?" Kent asked a few minutes before the bell rang.

"Here, look." Gene handed the paper to Kent, who read it over to himself:

Inventory complete. I will have list delivered _____ you tomorrow. _____ _____ greater quantity _____ estimate. _____ ready _____ move 2 weeks. We _____ send _____ long-distance telephone railroad. Please provide instruction _____ ____ date and location.

Kent and Gene were baffled by the patchwork of translated words interspersed with those they could not translate, particularly since they had no context for the message. They did not know its author, purpose, or subject matter. It appeared to be part of an ongoing exchange with many critical facts within the knowledge of only the intended recipient.

"How are we going to get the rest of this figured out?" Gene asked.

"I suppose I could give it to one of the students studying Russian. That would save a lot of time and be more accurate."

"But we can't let other people know what we're doing," Gene insisted.

"I'll tell him it's part of a game, like a scavenger hunt sort of thing with coded clues. He isn't going to know it's for real."

The bell rang, and the pair returned to class. Kent could remember the last name of the student who had given him the keyboard template—"Thompson" had been written on his notebook. "Damn, what was the first name?"

After school, they went to Kent's house and looked in the UW student directory. "There's about twenty 'Thompsons' here," Kent said, exasperated. "Maybe it was 'Richard.'"

Kent picked up the phone and dialed the number. "I got voicemail." A deep voice on the other end had said, "This is Rick, I can't. . ."

Kent hung up the phone. "Wrong Thompson. Voice doesn't match. Let's try Bryan. That sounds kinda familiar." Kent dialed the phone again.

"Hello?" The higher pitched voice sounded distinctive.

"Bryan?"

"Yes."

"Hi, this is Kent Dalton. I'm the guy who copied your keyboard template in the language lab this morning. I was wondering if you could translate a couple paragraphs of Russian for me. I'll pay you."

"Well, I haven't been studying Russian all that long. What do you need it for?"

"It's sort of a game I'm playing with another guy. The Russian messages he's given me are like clues. I'll pay you ten bucks an hour."

"How soon do you need it done?"

"Right away, if possible. Can we get together this evening?"

"Uh, yeah, I suppose. Do you want to meet at the main library?"

"Sure. Meet you by the front desk. How 'bout 7:00?"

"Seven will work. I'll see you then."

Kent and Gene were waiting at the library by 6:45 p.m. Bryan showed up twenty minutes later.

"Hi Bryan, I'm Kent and this is Gene. Why don't we go to a quiet corner, and I'll show you the stuff." Bryan and Gene followed as Kent led them to a table tucked away in the stacks. The three sat down.

"Here's the second message," Kent said. We started translating that one first. Here's what we came up with using a Russian-English dictionary."

"Hmm. This note is hard to read. A lot of the letters don't look right."

"I rewrote the message, and I wasn't sure how to write Russian characters. Sorry."

"That's okay. I think I can figure it out. It looks like you got your translation wrong on a few words. Close, though. This is 'estimated,' not 'estimate.' Um, this isn't 'telephone'—it's referring to a train that travels between cities as opposed to, uh, like a trolley within a city." Bryan continued to study the note. "Hold it."

"What?" Kent asked anxiously.

"Okay, you have the first couple sentences basically right. This third sentence though—let me check something." Bryan pulled out a much bigger Russian dictionary than the little paperback Kent had. "Yeah, that's what I thought," he whispered to himself. "This says that the stock of plutonium is in a greater quantity than estimated. What's this all about?" Bryan asked.

"I told you, it's a game with a friend of mine. He's at Beloit College. The game is a world domination thing. Come on, what's the rest of this say? I'm paying you by the hour, you know."

Bryan shot Kent a quick scowl and looked down at the paper again. "Okay, 'the materials can be ready to move in one week. We will need additional containment units from Moscow. Once those have been obtained, we can ship by rail. Please provide instructions as to date and destination.' It's 'destination,' not 'location.'"

"Write that all down so I don't forget," Kent instructed. I hope you can do a few more of these. I can have another one ready for you tomorrow. I'll continue to pay you ten bucks an hour."

"Okay, but I charge a minimum $10 per message even if it doesn't take an hour. Next time you can just drop the message in the mail or whatever rather than us taking time to meet at the library."

"How 'bout if I e-mail it to you in Microsoft Word format in that Russian font you were using?"

"Yeah, that's fine. My e-mail address is b_thompson."

"Great. Thanks for your help. My friend is going to be freaked when he realizes how quickly I figured this out. He probably thought it would take me months." Kent looked at Gene, and they both smiled. Kent then reached in his pocket, pulled out a crumpled $10 bill and handed it to Bryan. "Here you go. We'll see you around."

Kent and Gene left the library and stepped into the cold, evening air. "Why would Nick pay us thousands of dollars to find out that a plutonium inventory had been completed?" Gene asked.

"That's what I wondered. Why don't you walk with me over to the language lab. I'm going to copy the Russian font onto disk so we can convert the gibberish right into Russian by merely changing the font for the document. Then all we have to do is print it and get it translated by Bryan."

"Is there such a thing as a plutonium futures market, like for other commodities? Maybe Nick wants to know about the inventory to get inside information for trading purposes. They do have some sort of stock market in Russia now, don't they?"

"I don't know. I've never heard of a plutonium futures market. Maybe Nick is part of Russian law enforcement or the Russian equivalent of the Department of Energy. It could be they're concerned about safety violations—trying to prevent another Chernobyl. It might not even have anything to do with plutonium. Maybe the guy is just sleeping with the Energy Minister's wife. They probably don't have restrictions on government wiretapping and such over there. For that matter, maybe it's just routine monitoring, kinda like having cameras in stores to watch for shoplifters."

"We should have a lot better idea what this is all about after we get the other messages translated. Nick should know what the context is. We can send the translation to him right away."

Kent walked silently for a moment. "No, I think Nick already knows what it says. He must be Russian, and he must know what format it's in. I bet that's why he keeps sending us more messages."

"If that's the case, then we're getting ripped. He's cut our payment by letting us believe he couldn't read what we cracked. Let's tell him that we know what's going on and that we expect to get paid the full price."

"If he thinks we can't read these messages, we might be able to use that against him—beat him at his own game. We can get the translation before he does now. We just gotta find out what this is all about and how we can cash in on it."

"Ooo, that's a good idea," Gene said as his face lit up.

When Kent arrived home, he installed the Russian font on his computer and pulled up the first message with the Word program. He changed the font, and instantly the message changed to Russian. He saved the document in this format and e-mailed it to Bryan.

Late the following afternoon, Kent had the translation waiting for him when he checked his e-mail.

> Minatom [Russia's Ministry of Atomic Energy] has ordered us to conduct a thorough inventory of all sites storing bomb-grade nuclear materials. Prepare a detailed report within one week. Include specifications for transport of such materials to a new site and the time needed to have materials ready to move.

Kent printed the message, then sent a reply thanking Bryan and letting him know that $10 would be mailed to him. Kent called Gene and read the message to him. "This seems to be the message to which the other one was responding," he explained. "It really doesn't tell us anything new other than to confirm that we're dealing with Russia's Atomic Energy Ministry."

Timothy S. Jacobson

CHAPTER EIGHTEEN

Mashhad Region, Islamic Republic of Iran

The old steam locomotive strained to escape those who pursued it while pulling a full complement of more modern freight cars. The heavy, iron coupling-rods that spanned from wheel-to-wheel appeared ready to snap as they cranked faster and faster. Steam spurted out from the engine in a loud staccato, but the vapor was quickly subsumed by the dry desert air while the soot and glowing specks from the coal fire raging in the belly of the engine lingered in a long trail floating over the stretch of jostling rail cars.

A burst of light shot down from a knoll as if from the center of the sun that was setting behind it. The projectile from an old Soviet RPG shoulder-fired weapon tore into the third car from the front and exploded with an ear-splitting boom.

The engine continued forward, dragging two and a half cars behind it as it rocked from side-to-side, nearly tipping over. Flames engulfed the half-car it pulled, and a shower of sparks sprang from where it scraped the tracks.

The rest of the train, having a shredded car before it, derailed and piled up along the tracks like linked sausages.

Huge pieces of steel hurtled through the air as ton-after-ton of rail car smashed together. One car, quickly uncoupling at both ends, jumped up and spun on its long axis like a log rolling down a hill.

Anton Pavlovich Potanin grimaced. He was 47 years old, with a crew cut, bulbous nose, tan, weathered skin, and a horizontal scar across his forehead. "I had hoped it would stop the train a little more cleanly," he said with embarrassment, standing atop the same knoll from which the RPG had been fired.

Nikolai Volkov wrinkled his brow and sighed. He had come to Mashhad to observe the progress with training. "This would be unacceptable with nuclear materiel," he said. "We'd contaminate the whole damn Republic, and there wouldn't be anything left to sell."

"You are right, of course," said Potanin, "but I think it's important to explore such contingencies. It also boosts the men's morale to have a big, moving target to blow up. It's almost as much fun as stumbling into a harem."

Volkov chuckled. "Yes, I suppose. At least the Iranians are paying for this experiment."

The pair crawled into an armored personnel carrier and drove down to the base camp. Upon arriving, Volkov reviewed the "troops," a group of mercenaries who mostly consisted of former members of the old Soviet and current Russian armies. They wore a hodgepodge of uniforms and civilian clothing, some with woodland camouflage, others with desert camouflage, and even a couple in blue jeans. Volkov was disappointed at not seeing a crisper, sharper unit, but noted their eyes burned with intensity.

When they completed the inspection, Volkov, Potanin, and three senior officers proceeded to a tent where they would be served dinner. As they entered, a lizard, which had taken refuge from the heat of the day under the edge of the tent, scurried out, causing one of the men to jump.

"Scared, Oleg?" chuckled Potanin.

Oleg's fright quickly turned to anger. "Damn reptiles . . . jumping out everywhere." Oleg, a brute with tree trunk legs, bulging arm muscles, big hands, almost no neck, didn't look to be easily scared.

"Last week I heard one of the men found a huge snake in his bed," Lev added.

"Snakes are a delicacy on the plate, but never in bed," Volkov observed. The men sat down, now queasy from wondering what dinner might be.

Potanin tapped his throat, indicating it was time to start drinking. He grabbed a bottle of ice-cold vodka and splashed some in five short glasses. He raised his in a toast: "To Nikolai Mikhailovich and a successful mission!" The other men raised their drinks, and Volkov nodded. Potanin immediately refilled the glasses.

Just then, a tidy, young man dressed in white stepped in with a tray of black caviar, crab salad, and smoked salmon, and placed it on a cheap metal table with folding legs, covered in a white tablecloth to disguise its humble construction.

"Looks delicious," said Ivan, one of the officers. "Our rations in camp haven't been quite that extravagant—no offense to General Potanin, of course."

Later, borscht was served, with the smell of cabbage overpowering the beets, beef, and other ingredients in lending its fragrance to the tent. After that, the men helped themselves to mounds of beef stroganoff. They topped the immense feast with jam pancakes and dishes of ice cream.

During the meal, the men exchanged stories of military adventures, exotic locations, and practical jokes they had successfully pulled, while they stuffed food in their mouths unconcerned with manners. The vodka continued flowing after the empty plates were removed.

During a rare lull in conversation, Volkov said, "Well, I have some matters to attend to tonight. But before you go, I have one last item of business to take care of." He reached behind his back where he'd holstered a small pistol. He pulled it out and aimed at Ivan's forehead. Ivan looked into the barrel with his young eyes; his body shuddered as he sucked in breath.

"I hope you enjoyed the meal." Volkov smiled and squeezed the trigger.

The back of Ivan's head exploded, blood splattering the occupants of the tent. Lev, one of the officers, watched in horror, jumping back with his chair as Ivan's body slumped toward his lap. The body struck the tent floor, feet kicking in a grotesque dance of nerves, and became still.

Two guards entered the tent, their AK-47s ready. Volkov holstered his weapon and, motioning with his head, told the guards to remove the body. "I want him left in the middle of camp on the ground. If animals find him, good."

Volkov sat down. "Sources informed me," he said, "Ivan had a loyalty problem, but that's okay. The problem is solved." Volkov felt a drop of blood drying on his cheek and, annoyed, wiped it off. "Now, where were we? We will meet tomorrow at 9:00 a.m. for our strategy briefing. I look forward to hearing your ideas. Your work is critical to our success." He nodded to indicate the men were dismissed.

They got up, still stunned, and walked into night air that had cooled considerably.

Volkov pulled out his laptop computer, set it on the table, and hooked a cable from it to his satellite-linked modem. He read several e-mail messages, firing out short responses by pecking at the keyboard with two fingers.

At 8:45 the next morning, showered and fed, Volkov was ready to be briefed. Potanin and his senior officers were ushered into the tent. "Gentlemen, please come in," Volkov said. "Sit down."

Potanin continued to stand as he set up an easel with a topographic map showing a rail route going past a Russian nuclear facility. "With your permission, I'll begin explaining the situation," he said.

"Fine."

"This map shows the Lomonosov facility near Ordzhonikidze. This is the rail line running past," he said, indicating with a pointer. "Our intelligence information leads us to believe they will be removing their entire supply of plutonium from this facility and transporting it by train under orders from Minatom. Security is tight around Lomonosov, but will be weakest during transport, particularly when the train passes through this rugged stretch of the Caucasus Mountains."

Potanin continued, "The primary difficulty with any plan of attack is having sufficient time. Trains generally pass along this line every three hours. If we intercept a train, it will be difficult to get the nuclear materiel off, then onto other transportation, and still have to deal with the captured train before another one comes along. If we leave a disabled train on the tracks, it will raise attention prematurely, making it more difficult to get the materiel out of the country.

"What we have done is locate a spot where the tracks level out, and where there is a thick, wooded area off to the side. Here we have laid a spur track behind the cover of the trees, bushes and artificial camouflage to within 20 feet of the existing tracks. A switch has already been installed into the rail line.

"When we know our train is coming, we'll have three hours, perhaps a little more, for our crew to quickly lay the last 20 feet of track up to the switch. When the train reaches that area, we switch it onto the spur and move it out of sight into the woods. If the removal goes quickly, we can back the train off the spur and send it on its way under a replacement crew to hold off suspicion for a longer period. If removal is difficult, we continue to work on it even after other trains have gone by, and we can abandon ours in the woods. As long as we maintain false communications with the government, they won't suspect their train is missing until it fails to arrive at the next station—five hours later."

"Certainly," Volkov said, "the government is going to have various electronic means of tracking the train. How do you plan to contend with this?"

"We've been able to determine the types of devices used to track such trains and the frequencies used. With U.S. funding, Russia recently upgraded security on the trains. There will be a GPS or global positioning system device on board. It will determine the exact location of the train at all times and transmit that information to Moscow. We'll be monitoring the train's GPS signal, and when we direct the train onto the spur, we'll jam its signal and send out a false one to look like the train is traveling uninterrupted.

"There also will be voice communications from the train. We'll jam those as well and issue false reports."

"How will the materiel be transported once the train is intercepted?" Volkov asked.

"Mi-8 helicopters will pick up the plutonium containment units. They'll be towed by cable below the helicopters. The helicopters are able to fly low and avoid radar. Vladimir Petrovich Stoletov, our smuggling expert, has worked out the details of establishing an air corridor over Azerbaijan and Armenia and getting it into Iran."

"I have concerns," Volkov said. "I'm going to mull these things over. We can meet again this evening."

Timothy S. Jacobson

CHAPTER NINETEEN

Madison

Six days after Kent had the last message translated, he received a new message from Nick with $2,000 simultaneously deposited as promised. Kent now had two PGP encryption keys from cracking the earlier messages. He tried both of them. The key used for the first message worked, and immediately decoded the message. Nick had no way of knowing that Kent could now decode such messages so quickly. Kent converted the text into the Russian font and e-mailed it to Bryan.

This time it took Bryan a day and a half to return the translated message to Kent. Kent read it while sitting in his bedroom at home after school.

> Here's the message I translated. The Kurchatov Institute it refers to is Moscow's scientific headquarters for Russia's nuclear program. The Russian *"mafiya"* is similar to the Sicilian Mafia. I hope this helps your game.

> A train will be made available to you November 16 and another one on November 21. You will ship the materials to the Kurchatov Institute. You will be responsible for providing security during transit. There is reason to believe the *mafiya*, particularly Nikolai Volkov's group, will attempt to intercept the shipments for sale to Iran for their nuclear weapons program. It will be necessary to take extreme precautions.

Nikolai? Could that be Nick? And the Russian *mafiya*? That would explain being paid thousands of dollars to crack messages, Kent thought. They must get paid millions for nuclear materials. Kent dialed Gene's number, but he wasn't home. Kent liked to eat when deep in thought, so he wandered downstairs and stared into the fridge.

"Kent, don't stand there with the refrigerator door hanging open," John scolded as he entered the kitchen.

"I'm looking for something to eat."

"If you have to contemplate your decision, you can do it with the door shut."

Kent rolled his eyes. "Yes, Dad." Here he was fooling the Russian *mafiya* and solving some of the world's most complex encryption problems, and his dad treated him like a little kid. He pulled out a package of cinnamon-raisin bagels and popped one in the toaster.

"How's school?" John asked.

"Fine."

"Just fine? Anything in particular of interest?"

"No. Same old stuff." Kent and his dad never really communicated; they just talked.

"I noticed you have a whole array of big backup drives on your PC now. Where did you get that?"

"I picked 'em up at PC Warehouse."

"That must have cost a lot."

"It was on sale. I had some money tucked away. With all the important software I have, I couldn't risk a hard drive failure."

"Well, I guess that's not a bad thing to have. I just thought you would mention it to me before you went out and spent all that money."

"I didn't think you would care. It's not like I spent the money on beer or something."

Just then the phone rang.

"I'll get it." Kent dashed across the room. "Gene! Let me move to the phone in my room. Dad, can you hang this up when I get upstairs?"

"Sure."

Kent carried his bagel upstairs to his room and picked up the phone. "I got it now, Dad," he hollered. Kent shut the door and heard the click of his father hanging up the other phone. "Gene, we got the last message translated. It sounds like Nick is in the Russian *mafiya* and that he's trying to steal plutonium to sell to Iran so they can build bombs."

"You're kidding."

"No, I'm not. This is for real."

"Holy shit! No wonder Nick paid so much for our services. What do you think we should we do?"

"We can't send this message on to Nick. He'll figure out what's going on and intercept the nukes. We have a chance here to stop the Iranian Ayatollah, or whoever's running the show, from becoming a nuclear power."

"I don't like the idea of withholding the message from a *mafiya* type."

"What can he do about it? We'll just say something went wrong."

"Then we piss him off, and we don't make any more money." The two sat in silence. "What if we send him a fake message? That makes Nick happy since he'll still think we're doing our job, and it makes us happy because we get paid and still save the world from a nuclear threat."

"What would we write?"

"I don't know. Maybe we could say that plans to move the plutonium are on hold. We just write some crap, then have that Bryan guy translate it for us."

"I suppose we could write something. We have a little extra time since Nick won't know the encryption has been broken. I'll start working on something here. Why don't you come over?"

"I'll come over as soon as I can."

By the time Gene made it to Kent's house, Kent had prepared a message, being careful to maintain a length that corresponded to the length of the actual message. Gene suggested some modifications. Kent called Bryan to ask if he would be willing to translate a message into Russian.

"Yeah, I could do that," Bryan replied. "But I'll need to charge $20 per hour for that kind of work. It's harder than translating Russian into English."

"Can you have it ready by tomorrow afternoon?"

"I think so." Kent e-mailed the message right after hanging up the phone.

The following afternoon, the translated message was ready for Kent. He switched it to a regular font and converted the binary file to ASCII text. Kent waited a day and e-mailed it to Nick with another apology for sending gibberish.

Kent got up from the chair at his computer desk, walked over to his bed and flopped on top of it. Maybe the proper authorities should be notified, he thought. Was it enough to merely withhold one message? What if Nick had other ways of learning about the impending transfer? Maybe Nick used the intercepted messages to confirm what he already knew. The first two messages would have tipped him off that a transfer was about to occur anyway.

But how do you tell the authorities you've been corresponding with the Russian *mafiya*, particularly when you're engaging in illegal use of thousands of computer systems to decipher messages that led you to know about the *mafiya*? And who do you tell? The CIA? The NSA? The FBI? Russian authorities directly? Perhaps he should just stay out of it. Maybe he would tell Nick he could no longer do any more deciphering. Sure, it had brought some easy money, but at what cost? He had inadvertently helped the *mafiya* already by supplying them with the first two messages, and it distracted him from working on MIPHSCI. He decided to sleep on it for a day or two, then discuss it with Gene.

Timothy S. Jacobson

CHAPTER TWENTY

Bushehr Nuclear Complex, Iran

Nikolai Volkov gazed out the window of his private Gulfstream jet, his eyes meeting the glistening waters of the Persian Gulf as the pilot decreased altitude. The plane swooped over the ancient port city and landed on the 10,800-foot runway.

Volkov mashed the smoldering butt of a cigarette into an ashtray, and stepped out of the plush vehicle accompanied by a bodyguard and a Russian nuclear physicist who had "taken a vacation" from the secret city Arzamas-16. They walked past a white Iran Air jet adorned with the Iranian flag on the side and the distinctive black logo of the airline on the tail. They were greeted in the terminal by a young bearded man who led them to a waiting car.

As they approached the German-built nuclear plant, bomb craters from Iraqi attacks in the 1980's came into view. The craters remained as silent motivators for the small group of nuclear scientists employed at Bushehr.

Inside the heavily guarded compound, Ahmad greeted Volkov with a vigorous handshake, and Volkov introduced his companion.

"It's so good that you came here," Ahmad said, looking from one to the other. "By showing you the extent of our progress in constructing nuclear weapons, we hope you can determine how best to fill the gaps. We've made significant progress despite a number of setbacks."

Ahmad gestured for the men to follow him on a tour. "We've mastered the uranium cycle. My country possesses large quantities of natural uranium, and we've developed three milling plants. We also have a plant for converting the yellowcake to uranium hexafluoride gas, but even with 5,000 centrifuges, our capacity is small, and it would take years to reach critical mass."

Volkov's nuclear expert nodded with understanding of the hurdles faced by the Iranians. "I'd be interested in touring your hex plant. We've made some significant technological advances in fluorification recently, and we may be able to apply them to your facility."

Ahmad's face brightened at the suggestion. "If you're available tomorrow, we could fly to Fasa." Ahmad led the men past a guard armed with a machine gun and entered a gray concrete building with no windows. "Our progress in constructing the elements of the bomb might surprise you."

They walked through an office area filled with cubicles buzzing with activity. Engineers and physicists manipulated 3-D drawings and columns of text on advanced computer workstations—American technology, Volkov noticed. They passed a control room with banks of lights, dials and knobs visible through a large window. They reached a storage room at the far end of the building. Ahmad closed the door behind them, and a wall opened up to reveal an elevator. Volkov assumed Ahmad used a remote control device to accomplish this. The elevator had been well concealed.

Volkov could feel the elevator taking them down, but he couldn't determine how deep they traveled. The heavy steel door opened into an expansive room in which white-coated people huddled around different work areas.

Ahmad waved his hand at the room before them. "The world knows of our underground enrichment facility at Natanz, but this one remains a well-guarded secret. We are under 300 feet of rock—well protected from airstrikes."

Ahmad guided them to another door, this one guarded and secured with a numeric keypad-controlled lock. He moved in front of the keypad and punched in the access code. The lock clicked open, and they stepped inside a small enclosure. In the middle of the room sat a sturdy rectangular table with a device, the length of a trombone case but three times as wide, resting on top.

The Arzamas physicist raised his eyebrows. "You've built it?" he said with incredulity.

"Almost. All we need is a plutonium 'pit.' We have other devices nearing completion as well. We're counting on you to fill the hole."

"I, and only I, have the ability to make your country a nuclear power within the next month or two," Volkov bragged, stroking the bomb casing with his hand. "Your government has had difficulty paying the Russian government for work done at Bushehr in recent years. I will not be as patient in waiting for compensation. Will you be able to pay the price?"

"Payment will not be a problem. It was hard to motivate the government to pay for incremental progress, but our leaders can taste success now, and their lust to achieve this goal for the Islamic Republic will open their wallets."

CHAPTER TWENTY-ONE

Madison

Kent sat in his bedroom thinking about Sam as he stared blankly at her computer science syllabus. He wondered how he could get a chance to be alone with her, to be undisturbed. With the tutoring sessions in her dorm room, it seemed that Sam's roommate, Helen, never left for more than two or three minutes at a time. Kent had the distinct impression that Helen purposely hung around during these sessions.

Kent let his eyes focus on the syllabus. The next section covered iterative functions. Kent's eyebrows popped up and he smiled. He had written several programs using iterative functions to draw beautiful computer graphics. They were programs set up to run on Kent's PC at home, and that is where he would have to show them to Sam to assist with "tutoring."

He reached for the phone, but stopped with his hand on the receiver. "What do I say to her?" he wondered. "She's gonna turn me down."

He let go of the phone and picked up a pen and notepad and began to outline what he would say. He changed his mind several times, filling the page with crossed-out lines. He thought ahead a few moves in the conversation, as if in a chess game, preparing to counter different possible moves by Sam.

He picked up the phone, hesitated for a moment, then quickly pounded out her phone number from memory. Kent didn't usually have anyone's phone number memorized after only a short time. Although intelligent, he tended to be absentminded.

"Hi, Sam," he said. "I was looking through your C.S. syllabus, and noticed the next section is on iterative functions. I have some great graphical programs at home that rely on iterative functions. I thought it would make it much easier for you to understand if you saw my programs. They're only set up to run on my computer at home, so you would have to come here to see them. I thought maybe you could come over tomorrow evening for tutoring. We could get some pizza."

"Well, I suppose. How about seven?"

"Yeah, seven is good. Okay then, see ya tomorrow."

Kent knew his father was scheduled for a meeting the following evening, and usually went out with other faculty for a few drinks afterward. John would probably not return home until 11:00 p.m., and that would give Kent four hours alone with Sam, if he could keep her there.

On Tuesday, John entered the house shortly after 5:00 p.m. Kent, in an effort to get his dad out as quickly as possible, had prepared a dinner of barbecues, French fries, and corn.

John entered through the kitchen door, stopped, and cocked his head to the side. "Are you sure you're feeling okay?"

"What do you mean?"

"Well, yesterday you cleaned your room, and today you've cooked dinner before I even got home."

"You act like I never do anything around here," Kent snapped.

"Hey, I was just kidding. Don't get so defensive. It smells good."

"It's hard to screw up barbecues." Kent stirred them again with a large, wooden spoon and shut the burner off.

"So, what did you do today?" John asked as he retrieved milk from the refrigerator.

"Not much. Just went to classes."

"Well, how's MIPHSCI been coming along this past week? I've been too busy to check with anyone on its progress lately."

"Good, really good. I finished the program to handle the distributive computing tasks through the UNIX network. I've run some tests by having it factor large numbers, and it's performed well. Now we need to fine-tune the integration with the hardware sensors. That's gonna eat up some major time training the neural net, but I think Stan and Phil are about ready to go with their end of that."

"Great. I'm glad to hear you're making progress, but I hope the time you're spending at UW isn't adversely affecting your grades in high school. You're still a student there too, you know."

"Yes Dad, I know. I'm doing fine."

At 6:30, John headed to his meeting. Seven o'clock arrived, but Sam hadn't shown up. Kent sat in the recliner in the living room listening to a Pearl Jam CD with the volume turned low so he could hear approaching cars. At 7:10, still no Sam. Maybe she'd decided not to show, Kent thought. He wondered if his directions had been good enough.

Kent started upstairs to check something on his computer. Halfway up the stairs, he heard a car door slam. He ran down the steps, his heart pounding, and peeked out the window. It was Sam walking from her 1992 Saab she'd parked on the street. Kent jumped over to the stereo, turned up the volume slightly, and plopped back into the chair pretending to have been there all along.

The doorbell chimed, and Kent rose from the chair and walked slowly over to the door, practicing being casual and relaxed. Kent looked through the glass in the door before opening it. Sam was looking over her shoulder, checking out the surroundings. Kent thought she must have the most beautiful profile of any woman he knew. A frosty breath escaped her slightly-parted, full lips and hung momentarily in the still, frigid air. Above the lapels of her black, mid-length leather coat, Kent could see she wore the same clingy, pink blouse she'd worn the first time he saw her.

"Hi, Sam. Come on in."

"Hi, Kent. Brrr! It's cold out tonight."

"Well it's warm in here."

"This is a nice house you have."

Kent figured Sam's house must be much nicer, judging from the furnishings in her dorm room.

"Are your parents home?" she asked.

"Ah, no. My dad's at a meeting on campus right now. I don't expect him back until about 11:00. My mom died ten years ago."

Sam bit her lip. "Oh, I'm sorry. I didn't know."

"It's okay. It was a long time ago. Have a seat. Would you like a beer?"

"Sure."

They drank Leinies and shared stories about their families. Later, Kent ordered a pizza and grabbed another beer.

"We should go upstairs while we're waiting for the pizza and start working on my computer," he said.

The pair walked up the stairs, Kent in the lead. He flipped on the light in his room, and Sam entered, looking all around her. An Einstein poster was taped above the computer, and posters of bikini-clad women and sports cars adorned the wall above Kent's bed. Kent noticed Sam looking at these, and suddenly became self-conscious thinking that the room must appear rather adolescent to her.

Sam's gaze next turned to a shelf in the corner near the computer, where sat a strange looking device she didn't recognize. "What's that?"

"What's what?"

"That thing on the shelf."

"Oh, that's my wireless telegraph." Kent stepped over to the shelf and pulled it down. "This part here is a replica of a Nineteenth Century telegraph. I made it myself. The wires leading from it are hooked to a modern FM transceiver that I also made. The transceiver saves me the trouble of running telegraph wires across the neighborhood to my friend Gene's house."

"Why on earth would you want a telegraph? What good is it?"

"Well, I use it for communicating with Gene."

"But why use a telegraph when you have a phone? Or is Gene stuck in the Nineteenth Century?"

"Sometimes I think Gene is stuck at the last ice age, but that's not the reason. It's just kinda fun communicating in Morse Code. You still need to do that to obtain certain ham radio licenses. Besides, older technologies are sometimes superior to modern stuff anyway."

"How can an old telegraph be superior to a phone?"

"Well, for example, if the phone lines are down, I can still use this. Did you know that until three years ago, the Chicago Fire Department dispatched all its fire trucks by telegraph, sometimes with thousands of calls a day? A decade earlier when Chicago tried to replace the telegraph with a high-tech radio dispatch system, it found the telegraph worked more reliably."

"You're kidding."

"No, it's true. A lot of older technologies are less vulnerable. Let me give you another example. The Russian MiG fighter jet is technologically backwards. It still uses vacuum tubes for all of its electronics instead of integrated circuits and such. In some ways, it's less reliable and certainly less sophisticated than our jets, but it's also much less vulnerable to an electromagnetic pulse which could emanate from a nuclear explosion in the event of war. The electronics on the planes of our military would be fried by a distant nuclear explosion in space, while Russia's jets would be largely immune."

"Alright already," Sam said. "You've convinced me. You can keep the telegraph."

"Why don't I show you some of those programs on the computer." Kent displayed stunning computer images and the programs that created them.

The doorbell chimed.

"The pizza's here. Good time for a break," Kent said as he fumbled for his wallet.

"Here's some money," Sam offered.

"No, no. I got it."

Kent paid the delivery guy and shut the door, locking it. He set the pizza down on the mahogany coffee table in the living room. "Can I get you another beer?"

"Sure, I'm ready for another one."

Kent grabbed his third beer while getting Sam her second. They watched TV while eating. Sam finished her second beer washing down pizza, and Kent replaced it.

When his bottle was half empty, he said, "Maybe we should go back upstairs and finish going over your C.S. homework."

The two walked back upstairs carrying beer bottles. Kent sat on the bed. "Come here, and I'll show you the program that drew those pictures."

Sam plopped down on the bed beside Kent to his left, and he showed her a printout of the program. After a few minutes of explaining how it worked, Sam felt a slight buzz, and she dropped backward onto the bed in a reclining position with her feet still on the floor.

"Boy, I think the beer hit me."

Kent dropped the fanfold computer paper on the floor and dropped back to recline alongside of Sam. "I think it hit me too," Kent said, studying every part of Sam's face. He let his eyes wander down to her breasts, watching them rise and fall with each breath she took.

He started to move his right hand over toward Sam and then stopped. She lay still, looking upward. He lightly grasped her hand. To his surprise, Sam squeezed lightly in return and rolled on her side to face him. Kent, summoning new strength and confidence, moved his face up to Sam's and kissed her. He quickly withdrew a little to see her reaction. He just as quickly moved in again and kissed her passionately. He had never kissed a girl like this before, and he wasn't sure if he did it right. But as Sam's lips tugged at his, he stopped worrying and kissed her with searing desperation.

His hand dropped hers and moved to the back of her hip, pulling himself against her. They continued to kiss while he caressed her. Then he eased his hand up to her left breast and lightly cupped it. He slowly shifted the position of his body in a gradual effort to move above her.

Sam's eyes opened, her mouth closed, and her body stiffened. Kent stopped. "What's the matter?" he asked in a whisper.

"I, I'm sorry. I gotta go." Sam quickly got up from the bed and flew down the steps, grabbing her jacket from a chair in the living room.

Kent stood at the top of the stairs. "Wait!" he pleaded.

"It's okay, I just have to go. I forgot about something," she replied without looking at him. She slipped on her coat but didn't fasten it. She tried to open the door and then realized it was locked. She turned the dead bolt and ran out into the night, shutting the door behind her.

"Shit!" Kent shouted through clenched teeth. He plopped down on the top step. "Now I've blown it."

Timothy S. Jacobson

CHAPTER TWENTY-TWO

Moscow

"We will soon have unprecedented wealth and power, billions in hard currency," Volkov announced as he slowly paced at one end of the room like a caged animal.

His audience was about a dozen men, members of the Russian *mafiya* who sat around an oval, gray marble table puffing on cigarettes in his penthouse apartment. Most of them wore Armani blazers and black turtlenecks with Rolexes adorning their wrists.

Three men stood around the perimeter of the room, Glock 9mm handguns tucked in shoulder harnesses inside their blazers. A 5.45-caliber Kalashnikov assault rifle rested against the wall behind one of them.

"It is your job to ensure we obtain this wealth even if it means leveling Moscow," Volkov continued. "We anticipate that our government will be consolidating certain supplies of bomb-grade plutonium in the next few months. As you know, there is a push from within Russia to reclaim its nuclear materials from the other republics and to maintain tighter central control that was fractured along with the Soviet Union. Already, President Kuchma in the Ukraine rid his republic of all nuclear weapons, and he accomplished this one month ahead of schedule. The West is also anxious to see this process completed and has provided funding to speed things up. With many nuclear depositories scattered and inventories still incomplete, there is no better time for us to act to intercept these materials."

Volkov's eyes narrowed. "Of course, we have an anxious buyer in the Middle East. The best time for us to strike is when the materials are in transit."

"How do you hope to accomplish this?" inquired Umov, an overweight, graying man in his late 40's.

"We have people on the inside at various nuclear facilities and at Minatom. They have been providing small quantities of nuclear materials and valuable information, but unfortunately not enough of either item. We have the personnel capable of performing a quick strike to steal the materials in transit, which will almost certainly be by rail. Anton Pavlovich Potanin here has done a fine job training his men for this assignment." Potanin sat stoically, his chest now inflated and his gut sucked in, smiling within to this rare praise from Volkov.

"What about moving the damn stuff out of the country? This isn't going to be as easy as our other smuggling jobs."

"Vladimir Petrovich in Georgia has worked hard to ensure our supply routes for export are kept open."

"I think this is the height of insanity," Umov complained. "There are a thousand different ways this could go wrong, and then we lose it all."

"We may be insane, but when we're done, we will be insanely rich. There are always obstacles to overcome. You do not get returns unless you are willing to accept risk. We have some of the finest minds in the world analyzing every angle. Our intelligence gathering is unsurpassed, and we have a secret technological advantage that I will describe to you when the time is right. Do you realize how ripe this fruit is? Two Octobers ago, Vladimir Nechai, director of the Chelyabinsk-70 nuclear complex, shot himself in shame over the failure of the government to pay scientists $50 a month. If we are going to do this, we must move while their morale is low and their management is in disarray. Do you have a suggestion for how we can get so rich so quickly without risk?"

Umov raised one finger from the table. "There is one possibility. Under the 1994 $12 billion 'Megatons to Megawatts' pact, Russia sells scrapped nuclear warheads to the U.S. to be converted into fuel, and Russia gets cash and natural uranium from American utilities. My sources have confirmed that AO Techsnabexport, the marketing arm of the Russian Ministry of Atomic Energy, is looking for a joint venture partner with high-level U.S. ties to complete the sale of the latest $1.5 billion installment. We could use our people in America to put together a joint venture proposal. We could turn a $150 million profit and leverage it by bidding for U.S. Enrichment Corp., an American government entity about to be privatized. USEC runs the world's two most advanced uranium enrichment plants. We could create a monopoly in the uranium markets."

"Interesting idea, but do you realize that American bureaucrats are going to be crawling all over those transactions like carrion beetles on a rotting carcass? The slightest hint of our involvement will cause the whole thing to crash. Primakov's people will also be impossible to deal with. They aren't going to do anything to jeopardize such an enormous cash transfer. It is ludicrous to think we can inject ourselves into such a public, highly-scrutinized process. The initial return would also be only a fraction of what we can take through sales of stolen materials. Once we have the cash from our sales to Iran, we will be in a much stronger position to buy our way into more visible deals." Volkov looked around the room. "Is everyone with me on this?"

Heads nodded around the table. Volkov looked straight at Umov who squirmed for a moment. "Da, I am with you," he responded at last.

"Okay then, you will meet now with Kirill Kardirov to get your individual assignments." Volkov paused for a moment before he turned and left the room.

CHAPTER TWENTY-THREE

Madison

The morning after having Sam at his house, Kent tried to avoid getting out of bed. He set his alarm clock for a half hour later than normal, and when it went off, he hit the snooze button several times. Finally his dad entered the room.

"Kent, get up!"

"Mm hmm," Kent replied in a barely audible tone.

John waited half a minute more, watching his son. "Kent, I mean it. You're going to be late unless you get moving right now."

"Yes, Dad." He weakly fought with the covers to untangle himself. When at last he had removed these, he rolled onto his back with a groan and opened his glazed eyes a crack and stared at the ceiling. Sleep had not come easy that night, but now it resisted departing.

Later, after Kent had dragged himself to high school and then to the university campus, he avoided Gene and Sam. He had to figure out a way to recover from this, but he didn't know where to start.

That evening, John arrived at home later than normal. Kent read a textbook in the living room, and John walked over to the couch and sat down.

"Kent, I received a letter from the Defense Department today. Apparently there's a lot of pressure from the top for them to cut costs. They want us to justify current expenditures on MIPHSCI and to report on our progress."

"They haven't given us enough time."

"No matter. We've got to prepare an interim report quickly, and I'd like some loose ends tied up before then. I've scheduled a meeting with our team in two days. That will give everyone a chance to figure out where they've been and where they're going. If you have time, would you be able to run through some training sessions with the neural net? I know you've been busy, but it would help if we could demonstrate some progress on that."

"Sure. I've come across some studies on motor activity prediction. I think we need to start simple with a large number of repetitive trials where the net will be trained to predict one of two possible movements of the arm. I don't think it will take MIPHSCI long to learn to anticipate a movement a couple tenths of a second before it occurs."

"Good. I'll let you schedule something with Phil and Stan. We've got another student lined up to be wired into the machine. We want someone who doesn't know anything about the objectives of the test."

"Why?"

"I know you like to be hooked up, but your physiological responses are likely to be altered by your knowledge of our purpose. Besides, we need you to fine-tune the software during the test."

"Dad," Kent whined, "it won't skew the results if I do it. The test is entirely objective, based on actual movements. MIPHSCI either predicts them or it doesn't."

"Like I said, we need you working on the software end of it. We've got a deadline to meet here." John turned and walked out of the room.

After a while, Kent got up and called Stan. Stan and Phil were planning to work on it most of the following day, and Stan expressed confidence they could run through an extensive amount of repetitive neural net training sessions over the course of the day. He assured Kent there would be plenty for him to do.

Timothy S. Jacobson

CHAPTER TWENTY-FOUR

Moscow

Nikolai Volkov burst into Kirill Kardirov's office. "What is this I hear about a shipment of plutonium that we missed?"

Kardirov's face had all color drained from it. "I just got word of it myself," he replied. "It was apparently only a partial shipment. There should be plenty left at that facility. As long as we can intercept the next shipment, we can still put a deal together with Iran."

"Plenty?" Volkov shouted. "We have already lost at least a billion euros. How is it we weren't aware? The last message we intercepted and cracked said all transportation plans were on hold for several months."

"I don't know. Perhaps the government is using disinformation to throw us off track."

"Why would they bother, unless they suspected their encrypted messages were being intercepted? They know we are after their plutonium, but they wouldn't have a reason to know we were reading their encrypted messages unless Boris Levovich has been discovered."

"I don't think that's possible. We monitor him with great care, and he has earned considerable respect in his agency."

"Is it possible our deciphered messages are being manipulated by the elusive Encryptomash?"

"He doesn't even know the messages are in Russian. We've only been paying him half because he doesn't know what they say."

"If he's smart enough to break the encryption, don't you think he can figure out what language it is? Maybe he realizes the real money is not in working for us. I know we can't break the encryption ourselves, but is there any way we can verify whether the deciphered messages correspond with the coded ones?"

"I'll check with our computer programmers right away. What if he *has* faked the messages?"

"Then locate him. Communicate with him and give him a short time to cooperate. If that doesn't work, I will have a chat with him face-to-face."

"Yes, Nikolai Mikhailovich. I will take care of it right away."

Volkov left the room, and Kardirov called their head programmer, a young man they had lured away from a Russian ministry office by offering a salary five times larger than he had been earning.

"Aleksandr, this is Kirill Ivanovich. I have a question. Is there any way we can verify whether the decoded messages received from Encryptomash are genuine? Can you compare them in some way with the coded messages?"

"It might be possible, but I'm not sure. The strength of public key encryption is that it is not easily subject to statistical analysis and comparison."

"Is there any other way we can check it, particularly the last message?"

"Maybe I should have mentioned it before. I made some grammatical corrections in the last message I relayed to you. When Encryptomash sent it to me, there were some elementary errors in verb conjugation and such. It seemed somewhat peculiar—mistakes like a child would make—but I didn't give it much thought."

"Did you see grammatical errors in any of the earlier messages?"

"No. Just in the last one."

"See what you can do to determine whether the last one corresponds with the encrypted message. We need the answer as soon as possible. A lot depends on you."

"Yes, sir."

Kardirov immediately called Volkov, who had left in his armored Mercedes, and reported what had been learned from Aleksandr.

"He knows," Volkov replied on his voice-encrypting cellular phone. "Proceed as we discussed."

CHAPTER TWENTY-FIVE

Madison

It was Thursday, 9:55 a.m., and Kent had just finished class at the UW. He walked over to Sewart Hall to check his e-mail and to mess around with a new graphics program he had downloaded from the Net.

As Kent entered the building, he walked past a biology lab where the smell of formaldehyde struck his nose, sickening him. He thought about the time he'd held a cold, dead, formaldehyde-soaked fetal pig in his hands in high school biology class preparing to dissect it. It wasn't the animal being dead that bothered him. His dad had taken him pheasant hunting in the countryside before, and even though his first kill saddened him, the warm blood running over his hands had been more tolerable than handling a stiff, cold, slimy fetal pig.

Kent took the stairs slowly, and entered the computer lab which housed MIPHSCI. He sat down at a computer workstation, but before typing in his user name and password, he decided to check on the campus computer account he'd set up for Sam the week before. He logged into her account. Since he'd been present when she set it up, he knew her password. He popped into her mail program, but no messages waited for her—just an old one from Kent that she had already read.

Then he decided to check her "out box," the repository for mail Sam had sent from her account. There were two messages: one that they had sent to Kent's address to test the account, and another to Sam's friend Christine. Without a second thought, Kent double-clicked on that mailbox entry to read it. The message popped on the screen:

> Chris,
> I finally got campus e-mail. You've been pestering me to get it. Kent set up the university account for me. At least he's good for a few things. I'm really getting sick of him though. He's such a geek. Once this semester is over and I ace my computer class, I'll never have to see him again. I can't believe that he still hasn't caught on that I let him hang around me so I can get through C.S. For someone as smart as he is, he sure is gullible!
>
> Speaking of guys, what do you think of Brant, that hunk in French class? I was just about ready to talk to him the other day when Kent showed up and ruined everything. I hope Brant doesn't think I actually like Kent—then he'll never talk to me.
>
> Write back! I'll see you later.
> -Sam

Kent read the message twice, swallowed hard and blinked. How could this be? Kent had been obsessed with her and truly cared about her. "That bitch!" he whispered to himself. "How could I be so dumb! She used me."

He knew he had to respond, but how? He thought about forwarding the message to Sam's computer science professor with a suggestion that she was cheating. Maybe she would flunk or otherwise be disciplined by the university. He turned that thought over in his mind with a feeling of great satisfaction, trying to picture Sam's face when confronted with her "over-reliance" on Kent. It seemed to be great revenge. But then Kent realized he would get in trouble for doing Sam's homework.

"I know! I'll. . ." Kent's words tapered off as he began to exact revenge. He started by pounding out another message to Chris. Sam had told Kent before about certain annoying habits Chris had. Kent decided to point these out.

Chris,
It's me again. You know, I've been meaning to tell you some things, but I never knew the right time. I guess now is as good a time as any. You have some really obnoxious habits. Sometimes I wonder why I even hang around you. You're even worse than Kent in some ways. For example, you have a really gross laugh—you sound like a hyena in heat or something. It's really embarrassing when you laugh in public when I'm around. You also do your hair and makeup in really stupid ways sometimes. It's no wonder you can never find

a boyfriend. A lot of your clothes look like my grandmother's too.

I hate to be so blunt, but I thought it would be better for you to hear it from me than to find out some guy said it.
-Sam

Kent laughed out loud. Next he wrote to Brant.

Dear Brant,
This is Sam(antha) from French class. I go by Dominique in class. I've wanted to tell you something for a long time, but I wasn't sure how. I'm sorry to say this, but you have really bad breath and your feet stink. Just a little helpful hint. -Sam

Then Kent logged out of Sam's account and into his own. He broke into the registrar's computer and proceeded to view Sam's transcript. "I'll just make a couple little changes—small enough where it will look like registrar errors and not intentional sabotage. He changed a plus to a minus and lowered an "A" to a "B."

While in the registrar's computer, he decided to check out some other transcripts. He'd noticed a cute co-ed with golden brown hair and deep brown eyes in his political philosophy class, and he wondered if she'd been a good student. "Not bad," he concluded. "She's got some good gray matter behind those pretty brown eyes. I wouldn't mind getting to know her better."

Kent then exited the registrar's computer. Rage burned within him, and he had an uncomfortable tightness in his throat, but he decided not to waste anymore time on her. He checked his e-mail, scanning the list of a dozen or so messages, looking at the senders' addresses and the "subject" lines. One immediately caught his eye—it was from Nick. Usually Nick left the subject line blank so that everything would be encrypted, including Nick's instructions and comments that accompanied every message to crack. This time, however, the subject line said, "URGENT - READ IMMEDIATELY." Kent ran the PGP program to decode Nick's message.

> Who do you think you are dealing with? I know that you did not send me the actual message. We also know where you are. You have 48 hours from Wednesday at 9:00 a.m. GMT to send the real message or we will come for you. Do not do anything stupid like going to the police. They will not be able to protect you. If you give us the message, we will leave you alone.

Nine o'clock Greenwich Mean Time on Friday—that is tomorrow morning at 3:00, Kent realized, less than 24 hours away. His heartbeat had raced when he read Sam's mail, but now it slammed into his ribs. A shiver ran down his back; his hands turned clammy. Somehow Nick had learned of his deception. Apparently the translation had been flawed. Could Nick really know where he was? he wondered. Kent knew that using "anonymous" e-mail could not guarantee anonymity, but it would take considerable resources and a concerted effort to track down the source of such mail. On the other hand, this was the Russian mafiya, some of whom may have been in the KGB. Such people could have compromised the security of anonymous remailer computers long ago for times such as this.

Kent exited the PGP program while leaving the threatening message remaining on his machine in encrypted form, not having saved it in plain-text form. He cleared the screen and stared at it as he sat slumped in his chair.

"Don't move!" someone yelled. Kent jumped and snapped his head to look over at the door. Two campus security officers had entered the room and were running toward him. They grabbed him and pulled him to his feet. The dean of student affairs, Donald Nielson, entered the room and walked over to the workstation.

"Trying to get revenge for something?" the dean mused as he turned toward Kent. "It's Mr. Dalton, isn't it?" The dean looked at the security officers. "Escort him to my office," he commanded.

Mr. Nielson walked over to the nearby classroom where John Dalton was teaching and summoned him into the hall. Whispering, Mr. Nielson said, "I think you had better come with me right now. It appears your son may have engaged in some serious misconduct. I'll explain on the way over to my office."

John stared blankly at Mr. Nielson for a moment, his eyebrows raised in disbelief. Then he went back in his classroom. "I'm sorry, students, but an emergency has just come to my attention. Class is dismissed now. I'll see you back here tomorrow. We'll wrap up today's subject then, but be prepared to go over the whole topic on the syllabus for tomorrow." Smiles broke out on some of the students' faces as they got up from their desks; others appeared more concerned and whispered questions about what the emergency might be.

John joined Mr. Nielson, and the pair walked silently out of the building. Once in the open air outside, John turned to the dean and said, "What's going on?"

"It's still subject to further investigation, of course, but we believe your son broke into the registrar's computer and altered some grades. We caught him moments ago working alone at the same terminal from which the grades had been altered just minutes earlier. Fortunately, we monitor the registrar's computer carefully, and we implemented a new security system last week. As soon as an unauthorized user entered the system, we were alerted and able to monitor the intruder's activities. John, you have been one of the shining stars on our faculty for a long time, and I felt I owed it to you to tell you right away."

"I don't know what to say. Kent certainly has made his share of mistakes, but it's hard to believe he would do something of this magnitude. There must be some explanation."

"I'm sorry, John. I wish this weren't happening."

The two of them arrived at the administration building and walked to Nielson's office. As they went past his secretary's desk, Nielson turned to her and said, "Sally, I don't want to be disturbed while we're meeting."

"Yes, Don," she replied. She glanced over at John, then quickly looked down at the stack of papers on her desk.

"Dad, what are you doing here?" Kent asked.

"I invited him here," Nielson said. "Please sit down, both of you." Nielson settled into his high-backed burgundy leather chair. John sat across the desk next to Kent.

"What's going on?" John demanded from his son. "I heard you were snooping in the registrar's computer. Is that true?"

"Well, I. . ." Kent realized they had detected his presence in the registrar's system, but probably had no idea that he had sent nasty e-mail to others with Sam's account. In Kent's anger, he had been sloppy, allowing himself to be caught. There would have been several ways to prevent detection or, at a minimum, to get out quickly so they couldn't figure out who had done it. Kent studied the pattern of the carpeting on the floor. "Yeah, I did," he said at last.

"And did you alter someone's grades?"

"Yes. I'm sorry."

"Why would you do that? I don't understand. I didn't raise you like that." A heavy silence hung in the air while Kent continued to look down, motionless. "Well?"

"It's a long story."

"You better start telling it."

A little while later, Nielson sent Kent out of the room with supervision by a security officer.

"John, it's clear that I have to take substantial action here. I have no choice but to expel your son. There may be further sanctions, but because of your position at the university, and my respect for you, we'll deal with this internally and not file a criminal report. Obviously, Kent's computer privileges will be revoked at the university. I ask you to see he doesn't try to gain access from his home computer."

"Thank you, Don. You can be assured Kent will not be accessing the computer system here. He's going to lose his cable modem. I'm so embarrassed about this whole thing. I'm truly sorry."

"No need for an apology from you. These things happen. Unfortunately, Kent's emotional maturity isn't up to the level of his intellectual capacity, and we all know about young, broken hearts. This whole thing is really too bad. I thought Kent's presence here had been such a positive thing."

John got up from his chair and shook Nielson's hand. "Thanks again."

John walked out to where Kent waited. "You're coming with me," he said. They left the building and headed toward John's faux wood-paneled Chrysler minivan.

"I'm really sorry, Dad."

John remained silent until they got to the vehicle. "Get in," he barked.

Once inside the minivan, John said, "I've never been so disappointed in my life. You are throwing away your future. I can't believe you didn't stop to think about the consequences of your actions. I don't need to tell you that what you did was wrong. You know that. If you don't have the common decency to avoid shit like that, I'd at least hope you would have the common sense to think about your future. You could also think about me and how this affects my employment here."

"Dad, I'm sorry. I don't know what else I can say."

"Well, this time sorry is not good enough. Not only are you being expelled from the UW, but also, I'm grounding you for an indefinite period of time, and I'm taking away your cable modem."

Kent's mind snapped back to the *mafiya* message threatening his life. He desperately wanted to tell his father what went on, but couldn't. John wouldn't believe him, particularly after what happened today, and he would get in more trouble for breaking into all those computers. "Dad, you can't take my Internet connection! I promise I won't connect with the university computer system, but I gotta have the Internet."

"You expect me to believe you won't access the university computer after what I learned today? Anyway, I don't care if you would or wouldn't—I'm still taking it away. I don't know what else to do with you. I don't think you appreciate the gravity of the situation. Your actions threaten your entire future, my standing at the university, and the funding for our research projects, not to mention the effect there would be on that young woman if you hadn't been caught."

"Dad, I just lost it. She was using me. She led me on and then totally humiliated me. I'm sorry."

The rest of the way home, John drove in stony silence, his gaze fixed firmly ahead. Kent turned his eyes out the side window, then straight down to the pavement below, watching it zip past—but he felt like they were getting nowhere.

Back home, Kent trudged upstairs to his room like a man sentenced to death, dropped onto his bed, and buried his face into the pillow, the thought occurring that perhaps it would be better to end everything now than to have the *mafiya* find him.

John came into the bedroom, disconnected Kent's cable modem, and took it and the phone out of the room.

After a minute, Kent shut the bedroom door, and flopped back on the bed face-up. "What am I going to do? I've got to find a way to communicate with the government and have these people stopped."

Kent lay there, his watch audibly ticking, ticking, his mind and pulse racing. After about an hour, the adrenaline waned and his thoughts became muddled. He drifted off to sleep. His mind passed the barrier between consciousness and sleep seamlessly, his dreams forming from a blurry continuum of his thoughts while awake.

In the dream, Kent sat in front of his computer, typing a long e-mail message to the CIA. He tried to explain the course of events in a convincing way. He felt confused and grasped for the right words, but they eluded him. Finally he was finished, and he reached for his mouse to click the "SEND" button on the screen.

The mouse cord suddenly wrapped around his wrist. He tried to pull his right hand free, but the cord tightened. He reached over with his left hand to free himself, but the cord entangled that hand too. The cord pulled him closer and closer to the computer, his face just inches from the screen now. The screen changed colors, turning brown and textured, the face of a furious bear filling it, protruding from the screen, its long, sharp teeth clenched and lips rolled back, hot, dank breath emanating from its slimy nostrils. Kent's face was drawn close, preventing his eyes from focusing on the bear.

He squeezed his eyes shut, straining his whole body back, the mouse cord cutting into his wrists. The bear let out a low, rough growl from deep within its throat, then said in a coarse voice, "How dare you fight me? You will pay with your life!"

"Daaaaddddd!" Kent screamed as he felt the bear's wet nose touch his cheek and a tooth graze his skin as the bear's mouth snapped shut. "Daaaaaadd!" Kent pulled back harder with his hands, and they snapped free with a jerk of his whole body.

He awoke with a spasm, having jerked his arms over his head in his sleep. He breathed hard and his forehead dripped with sweat. He sat up quickly and looked around the room. His computer rested on the desk innocently with the power off. He slid off the bed, inched over to the window, and peered out, seeing an elderly neighbor raking leaves. Kent looked at his watch: 1:38 p.m. He felt hungry, but chose to ignore it. There were more important things to attend to. He had to stop the *mafiya*.

He walked over to his desk and sat down. Uncharacteristically, he did not turn the computer on, but rather, reached in a drawer and pulled out a piece of lined paper and a pencil. He began to write, slowly at first, and then more quickly and urgently:

> Gene, Nick knows. He knows where we are and he is going to kill us if he does not get the actual message by tomorrow at 3:00 a.m. This is not a joke. I'm grounded and my cable modem and phone have been taken away.

You have to e-mail the CIA and get Nick stopped. E-mail anonymously and demand confirmation within 30 minutes. Use account name "smithb" password "clinker" at UW, but route through anonymous remailer. Send to geomcmil@odci.gov, cc: davcarey-@odci.gov. Inform them of what we learned, but do not admit our methods of obtaining this information and omit some specifics so we have some leverage with them. Use the same PGP signature that we posted on the encryption newsgroup so they can verify that we are Encryptomash. Demand immunity and immediate protection in exchange for specifics regarding nuclear security.

Kent slipped the note back in his drawer and quietly walked downstairs. His eyes were met by those of his dad. "I'm just getting a bite to eat," Kent said.

"I've canceled my classes for today and tomorrow to stay home until I decide what to do with you. Maybe I'll send you to work on your Uncle George's farm for a month or two. There probably isn't an Internet connection within 20 miles of his place."

Kent pulled the whole wheat bread out of the fridge and made himself a peanut butter and jelly sandwich. He poured himself a glass of milk and retreated upstairs to eat. Gene hadn't come home from school yet, so Kent could only wait.

Suddenly, he felt exposed. He yanked the curtains shut and sat on the floor to eat. He didn't want to make himself an easy target in case bullets started popping through the walls. A deepening fear engulfed him.

He left a corner of his sandwich on the plate and looked at his clock/radio to see the time: 2:07 p.m. It would be another hour before Gene got home. Kent tried to read the latest issue of *Wired* magazine, but he got constantly distracted by thoughts about what could happen. Even if he could stop Nick, the U.S. government would learn all about Kent's numerous illegal activities. He would be watched like a hawk the rest of his life ... if he lived past tomorrow. He also could never feel safe from the *mafiya*. Even if he ended up in jail, the *mafiya* could track him down and have him killed.

Kent shifted his gaze around the room until it settled on the computer. "Damn machines," he thought. "Maybe I would be better off if I had never seen one." He thought about smashing his computer, ripping the cords out, blowing the monitor apart with some of his homemade explosives, crushing every fragment with a sledgehammer, burning the residue with an acetylene torch, vaporizing it all.

Then he thought about Sam. He wanted to do the same to her for betraying him, destroying him. He wanted to crush her skull.

Kent shuddered. "What has become of me?" he wondered. "I've turned into a beast. I am worse than worthless. I had a promising future. Now I have nothing but pain. Dad's career, my life—was it worth all that to get revenge?" Kent pulled his knees toward himself and dropped his head against them and began to cry. His crying became louder, and he sobbed violently. "Why? Why?" he pleaded out loud between choking sobs. "How could I be so dumb and so arrogant?"

After a while, his crying diminished. He felt cold. He rose from the floor, crawled under his bedspread, and huddled there. Finally he drifted off to sleep.

Kent's eyes popped open. He rubbed them and his cheeks too because the skin had puckered from the dried-on tears. He wondered how much time had passed, and glanced up at his clock/radio: 2:51 p.m. Gene would soon be home. Kent wanted to stay curled up under the blanket where it felt warm and safe. He shut his eyes, remembering his mother tucking him in on cold winter nights and sitting alongside him on the bed. He could see her warm smile, and hear her voice saying "good night." Kent half smiled now too. Then he thought how disappointed his mother would be, and the smile vanished.

He tried to reach Gene, clicking down on the wireless telegraph, hoping to get his attention. No response. Unlike the telephone, no easy way existed to get his friend's attention with the wireless telegraph, because no ring would alert him, just gentle clicking heard only in Gene's bedroom. Kent would have to keep trying every minute or two.

One advantage of the telegraph, other than it being his only means of getting a message to Gene: Kent felt reasonably secure Nick would not be able to intercept messages sent by this means.

Timothy S. Jacobson

CHAPTER TWENTY-SIX

London

Volkov stepped across Bruton Street and up to the entrance of Holland & Holland.

As he entered, a small, balding man said, "May I help you, sir?"

"Yes. I'm Volkov. There should be a .700 Nitro Express waiting for me."

"Yes, of course. Welcome Mr. Volkov. Please follow me to the Brevis Room."

Once there, even Volkov was amazed by the extraordinary collection of antique, hand-crafted firearms. His elderly guide offered a glass of Balvenie single-malt Scotch that Volkov accepted without hesitation. The gentleman excused himself from the room.

"You must be Nikolai Volkov," came a voice from the other direction. Volkov turned from examining a finely engraved shotgun to see a man younger than the first. "I'm George Smith, chairman and chief executive of Holland & Holland. I understand you have purchased a .700 Nitro Express," he said as he gave a firm handshake.

"Yes, I am anxious to see it. It's been a long couple of years since I ordered it."

"I believe you'll find it worth the wait. They are quite the rifle—biggest shoulder-fired weapon in the world, with the exception of LAW's, RPG's, and other dreadful military weapons."

"I have an appreciation for those too. It's hard to match the feeling of power when firing an RPG."

"I'm sure you're right. Bloody noisy, though. I would be a bit more comfortable dropping a rhino with a Nitro Express than hunting a tank with an RPG."

The elderly gentleman returned with a large, wooden box and eased it to rest on a table. He lifted the hinged lid. "Here it is, Mr. Volkov."

Volkov scrutinized the weapon, smiling at the beautiful engravings and gilding on the steel and the finely-crafted walnut stock. He slipped on a pair of white gloves that accompanied the gun to avoid leaving corroding fingerprints, lifted it like a fragile egg, put it to his shoulder and looked down the barrel, taking aim at an oil portrait on the wall.

"Just don't shoot Harris Holland in the picture. He founded this company in 1835," Smith said with a chuckle. "I hope you have the time to take it to our shooting grounds in Middlesex. We have 60 wooded acres. You can have lunch in the Pavilion there."

"Yes, I'd love to," Volkov replied, anxious to see if his $150,000 had purchased a weapon as accurate as it was elegant.

After the trip to the shooting grounds, Volkov returned to the heart of London and entered the Dorchester Hotel, carrying only a black leather duffel bag. He liked traveling light. At the front desk, he said, "I have reservations for tonight." A gold crown on one tooth twinkling as he spoke. "Nikolai Volkov."

"Yes, Mr. Volkov. You have room 649."

"What side of the building is that on?"

"That's on the north side."

"I'm sure that when I made reservations, I specified that I was to have a room on the south side.

I like to see the sun." Volkov never took the first room offered, for security reasons.

"I'm terribly sorry about the mix-up. Let me see. Room 904 is available on the south side. Will that

be okay?"

"That should work."

"Will you be paying by credit card?"

"Cash." Volkov pulled a wad of bills from the breast pocket of his suit coat and handed some to the desk clerk. His bag was picked up by a bellhop who led on to the elevator.

Volkov inspected the room, both visually and by means of an electronic bug sweep, then sat on the edge of the bed and placed a call.

"Kirill, this is Nikolai. Has our friend provided us with the decrypted message yet."

"No, we haven't heard a thing."

"Damn! Have you received confirmation yet on his location and identity?"

"We believe the messages are coming from the United States, from the University of Wisconsin in the City of Madison. We have the account name, encrypto-

@students.wisc.edu, which, of course, suggests it is a student there who is responsible. I don't know how you'll identify the specific student, though."

"Leave that up to me. It won't be difficult to convince the university administration to provide me with information once I tell them I am a member of their government and that it's a matter of national security. They just won't realize which nation's security is at risk. Make the appropriate reservations for me to get there tomorrow."

Madison

Kent repeatedly tried to contact Gene by telegraph. More than an hour and a half had gone by with no success. Kent's feeling of desperation increased. Gene was *always* home this time of day. Gene didn't participate in any extracurricular activities, and didn't really have other friends he hung out with after school. Usually, if not with Kent, he would be home satisfying his craving for munchies and watching TV, playing video games or tinkering in the garage.

Kent went downstairs where his dad was reading in the recliner. "Dad can I quick use the phone. . ."

"No!"

"But Dad, I just wanted to call Gene and let him know I'm grounded."

"I said no. Don't you understand the word? If Gene calls, I'll tell him you're grounded."

Kent turned around and trudged upstairs. He knew from the tone of his father's voice that he wouldn't change his mind. He tried again with the wireless telegraph. No response.

While Kent tried in vain to reach Gene, Gene puttered in the garage working on his bike and listening to a Metallica cassette.

"Gene . . . Gene!" his mother yelled from the kitchen. "Where is that boy?"

"I think he's out in the garage," said Gene's younger sister, Tammy.

Mrs. Fisher stuck her head in the garage and saw Gene hunched over the workbench facing away from her with the music from the headphones audible even from halfway across the garage. She called out her son's name again, but he did not respond. She walked up behind him and tapped his shoulder.

Gene jumped and spun around. "Oh, it's you. What do you want, Mom?"

"Turn that music down before you break your eardrums."

"Oh, Mom."

"Go up to your bedroom. A couple of times I heard a clicking noise from one of your contraptions."

Gene hurried inside. He pulled the junk off the top of the wireless telegraph and blew the dust off. He clicked down on it a few times.

Kent, lying on his back in bed, rolled onto his side and responded. "Gene, is that you?" he tapped out in Morse code.

"No, Santa." Gene replied.

Kent ignored the crack and responded with his pre-prepared message. "You still there?" Kent asked, after sending the message.

"Yeah. What do I write to the CIA?" Gene tapped out to Kent.

"You have to figure it out on your own. We are never going to get done in time using the telegraph. Let me know when you finish and when you get a response."

Gene sat for several minutes, then flipped on the aging computer he had picked up at a garage sale two months earlier and accessed the "smithb" account at the UW.

Gene rested his head on his hands and stared at the computer screen. "I don't know what the hell to write," he said to himself. "Why the heck didn't Kent figure this out. He's the one who got us in trouble in the first place."

Gene stared a little longer. Then he began to type the e-mail message. After completing three sentences, he deleted it all. Several minutes passed before he tried again. When he started writing a second time, the words flooded out of him like a murderer unburdening his soul with a confession.

Gene's telegraph started clicking: Kent inquiring whether the message had been sent yet. Gene replied,

"Almost done." A few minutes later, he'd finished. He clicked on the "send" button and hoped he would get a positive response. He let Kent know the message had been sent.

CHAPTER TWENTY-SEVEN

CIA Headquarters, Langley, Virginia

"What's this?" Paul Burrell asked his secretary as he looked at a printout of Gene's message.

"It's e-mail sent to the Director and the Deputy Director," she replied. "Shirley forwarded it down here for you to deal with.

Burrell read it over. "Interesting," he said. "How long have we had this?"

"I don't know. Doesn't it give the time at the top?"

"Yeah, it's been sitting around for twenty minutes and this guy is demanding a response in thirty. I think he's gonna have to wait a little longer. Why would Shirley send this to me? This doesn't seem to have anything to do with Latin America."

"I don't know. You just happened to be around. She also said something about you dealing with a similar situation lately. Do you think it's a prank?"

"Probably. It's anonymous. Most of them are. On the other hand, this person has done some research. He knew the e-mail addresses for the two top dogs here. Something else too—this 'Encryptomash' thing. I heard about that a while back. I'm going to run this by a few people."

Burrell dialed a coworker's extension. "Chuck? Yeah, this is Paul Burrell. Could you come up here right away? I want to show you something." He located a number in the agency directory and dialed again. "Hi, is Denise there? Yeah, I can hold a minute." Burrell sat with his head propped up by his left arm looking intently at the e-mail message.

After a moment a woman responded on the other end of the line.

"Denise? This is Paul Burrell upstairs. Have you been looking into that 'Encryptomash' thing? Yeah. Would you bring up what you have right away? We've just received e-mail from someone claiming to be that person."

Chuck, a man on the heavy side, sporting a neatly-trimmed beard, arrived a moment later. "What's up?" he asked.

"Just a second. Let me run off a couple copies of this." Burrell went to the photocopy machine nearby and fed the document through. He handed a copy to Chuck, who read it carefully.

"What do we know about the author?" Chuck asked.

"Not much. We don't know where it originated, but I think our people have been following communications from this 'Encryptomash' character for some time. Denise from our computer geek department is coming up to tell us what she has."

"Hey, I heard that!" Denise said.

Burrell turned and looked sheepishly at her. "Denise. Have you met Chuck? He's an analyst dealing with Russian nuclear security issues."

"No, I don't believe I have," she said, shaking Chuck's hand. Denise hardly looked like a geek. Young—in her early twenties—professionally dressed, attractive, with long, straight red hair and light blue eyes.

She turned to Burrell. "Where's the message, and what does this have to do with nuclear security?"

Burrell handed her the other copy. "Take a look."

"On the face of it," Denise said, "it appears to be the same person or group of people, but it could be an imposter. I'll have to run this through the computer to validate the authenticity of the message based on the PGP signature. Of course, that will only tell us if it was written by Encryptomash. We don't know who that is. We just have a profile."

Chuck looked puzzled. "What is this about Encryptomash, and why have you been following his communications?"

"It appears that someone, probably an individual, has figured out how to crack strong encryption. This person has been posting results on the Internet. No one else has come even close to his capability with respect to decoding public key encryption. It's a very high priority of the agency and the NSA to acquire this technology. Undoubtedly, Encryptomash has been approached by countless governments and criminal organizations worldwide offering to buy the technology. If it gets in the wrong hands, it could be destabilizing."

"We've considered that type of scenario for quite some time," Chuck said. "If this guy really has been providing the Russian *mafiya* with access to this technology, who knows what could result."

Denise looked at Burrell. "Can I log out of your computer account and into mine to authenticate the PGP signature on this?"

"Sure."

Denise turned back to the computer and began to type, her fingers a blur. She pulled up the PGP program and compared the two signature files.

"It's Encryptomash," she announced.

"How do you know it's not an imposter?"

"It's impossible to fake an authenticated PGP signature, that is, of course, unless you have Encryptomash's technology."

Burrell said, "There is still no way of knowing if the guy is just jerking us around. Maybe he wants to see if he can trick us into chasing him."

"That could be, but can we take that risk?" Chuck asked. "If we don't bite, the *mafiya* might get away with a nuclear heist, nuclear materiel might reach terrorists' hands, and Encryptomash could be killed before we learn his technological secret."

Burrell said, "Denise, do we have a profile on this guy?"

"Well, your stereotypical use of the term 'guy' is probably correct. It certainly could be a woman, but statistics disfavor that idea. We suspect he is young, between 20 and 35 years old. Probably a loner, although he might draw on the assistance of others. We don't think one person could have developed this capability totally on his own. It may be a network of people collaborating over the Internet. The lead person is probably a graduate student in mathematics or computer science. I'd guess it's someone like the guy who shut down the Internet back in the 80's with a worm program."

"Chuck, what's your recommendation for approaching him?" Burrell asked.

Chuck thought for a moment. "Here's our chance to get technology that could set us light years ahead of other intelligence agencies worldwide. If this is some student who tangled with the wrong people and now comes running to us for aid, I think we should sound inviting and willing to help, and milk as much information as we can. Respond immediately with e-mail requesting his location and identity so we can offer assistance. Maybe we should touch base with the Russian government and try to confirm things on their end."

The meeting ended and Burrell prepared to leave work for the day. He replied to the e-mail message and left behind instructions with an evening staffer for handling a call from Encryptomash in his absence.

Madison

About 75 minutes after he sent his message, Gene received a reply from "burrell_p@odci.gov":

> Your message is most interesting. However, without more information, there is nothing we can do for you. Tell us who you are, and where, and provide us with a telephone number so we can call to discuss this and perhaps arrange a meeting. You can call me at (703) 555-3620. -Paul Burrell

Gene immediately relayed the information to Kent via telegraph with the question, "What do we do now?"

Kent told Gene to ride his bike to a pay phone at least a mile from his house, wear gloves so as not to leave fingerprints, and place a call to Mr. Burrell for the purpose of setting up a meeting between Gene and the CIA.

By the time Gene made it to an outdoor pay phone a good distance from his house, it was almost 7:30 p.m. on a cold, clear, moonless night. Gene shivered despite the exertion of the bike ride. He didn't know if the shivering resulted from the temperature or nervousness. Gene got off his bike, walked up to the phone booth, and pulled a scrap of paper with the phone number from his pocket. He called the CIA collect. The phone rang again and again.

"What am I going to do if nobody answers?" Gene wondered.

A fourth, fifth, sixth and seventh time it rang. Finally, someone picked it up.

"Central Intelligence Agency. How may I direct your call?" a grumpy-sounding, middle-aged female mumbled.

"You have a collect call. Caller, please state your name," the computer operator said.

"Uh, Encryptomash," Gene stuttered.

"Will you accept the charges?" the computer inquired. "Please state 'yes' or 'no.'"

"Yes," the receptionist finally replied.

"Uh, I'd like to speak to Paul Burrell, please," Gene stated in a deeper than normal voice.

"Who's calling?" the grumpy woman inquired.

"Encryptomash. Mr. Burrell is expecting my call."

"One moment," the receptionist said suspiciously.

After about a thirty-second wait, another voice popped on the line.

"Paul Burrell's desk," a female voice stated.

"Could I speak to Mr. Burrell?"

"He's gone for the day. Is there something I can help you with?"

"No, I need to talk to Mr. Burrell. He was expecting my call. Well, *maybe* you can help me. I need to set up a meeting with Mr. Burrell right away."

"You said Paul was expecting your call. If you could tell me what this is about, maybe I could help you."

"I e-mailed Mr. Burrell today about an urgent problem I have with the Russian *mafiya*. He said I should call so we could discuss it."

"Does this have something to do with computer messages that were intercepted?"

"Yes, we've been deciphering messages for someone named Nick, and we now believe he's with the Russian *mafiya*. He has threatened to kill us by Friday at 3:00 a.m. Central Time if we don't turn over the most recent message which contains information about a nuclear transfer. You've got to help us."

"Okay. I can help you. You need to give me some information. Where are you?"

"Madison."

"Wisconsin?"

"Yes." It occurred to Gene he had been on the line probably long enough for them to trace the call.

"We can't protect you unless you give us a specific address."

"Look, I gotta go. Can you get someone here in Madison by tomorrow morning at 10:00? We can meet and discuss this."

"If you're in imminent danger, you should contact the local police immediately."

"No, I can't do that." Gene was convinced the police wouldn't believe him and wouldn't know how to respond to the situation. "If you can get someone here, we can meet at the Denny's restaurant at the corner of Main and 32nd Street tomorrow. Have Mr. Burrell or whoever come in carrying a Washington Post in his right hand. I will find him. I've gotta go." Gene had seen this done in the movies, and he had a cousin, Elaine, a waitress at Denny's, to help him out if needed.

"Wait . . ."

"Is someone going to be there or not?"

"I can't promise you anything, but we'll try to send someone there."

Gene hung up and sped away on his bicycle, taking a tortuous route home to avoid detection.

Kent had been trying to read *Wired* to make the time pass more quickly while he waited for Gene to complete his mission. The pages turned slowly as Kent's mind wandered. "Maybe I could send another fake message to buy some time, but what would I tell them?" he thought. He looked at the clock and wondered why he hadn't heard from Gene yet.

He tried to read some more. Again, he looked at the clock, but only four minutes had passed. The telegraph started clicking. Kent dropped the magazine without marking his page and jumped off the bed. He took down Gene's message on a scrap of notebook paper rescued from the wastebasket. "They will not commit, but someone might meet me at Denny's tomorrow at 10," it stated.

Kent typed a reply. "We can't rely on that. We could end up dead. Go ahead and send the actual message to Nick. The damn Russian government should be able to take care of itself."

Timothy S. Jacobson

CHAPTER TWENTY-EIGHT

The following morning at 8:40, Volkov landed at the Madison Airport, having missed the opportunity to enjoy his stay at the Dorchester. He exited with his black leather carry-on.

Volkov entered the first men's room he found and pulled a rechargeable electric razor from a side pocket on his bag. He had not shaved in 30 hours, and had to lose the heavy shadow on his jaw before heading over to the university. As he leaned toward the mirror, he looked into his own eyes, and a devious smile spread across his lips. "Yes," he thought, "I'm going to get that son-of-a-bitch. I'm going to teach him a lesson he'll never forget." After shaving, he put on a dark blue, conservative tie and buttoned down the collar on his white oxford shirt. Then, even though his vision was perfect, he pulled out a pair of round, wire-rim glasses with gold frames and perched them on his nose.

He left the bathroom and walked over to a bank of pay phones where he called Kirill to check for new developments and to report his arrival in Madison.

"We received a new message from Encryptomash. It purports to be the real message we intercepted, but we won't know until the events come to pass. If it's correct, then it came just in time. It speaks of another shipment to occur mere hours from now."

"Can we be ready?"

"We will."

"Excellent. Proceed. I'll finish my business here. I'm going to teach a lesson and take the technology for ourselves." Volkov hung up and strolled over to the car rental counter.

"How can I help you?" a chubby young woman asked.

"I would like a dark green Pontiac Grand Am, if that is available." Volkov would have preferred a bright red one, but that would be too conspicuous.

"Well, let me see . . . Ah, you're in luck. We have one left."

With the map obtained from the car rental desk, Volkov drove toward the university on the one-way exit from the airport. Having just been in England, he had to think whether he could remain in the left lane after the road turned into two-way traffic. "It is so damn ridiculous to not have a uniform way of driving in all parts of the world," he thought.

Volkov stopped at a McDonald's on his way to the university and ate pancakes and sausage washed down with black coffee. While eating, he studied the city map more carefully.

While Volkov munched his pancakes, Gene and Kent sat nervously in their United States history course at the high school. Kent often dozed off in this class, but today he stayed wide awake.

They discretely passed notes back and forth during the entire class period regarding how to deal with the CIA and what to communicate in the event they showed up. Then the bell rang, marking the end of class, all too soon for Gene. He had an hour between History and his next class, when he would meet with the CIA. The high school had an open-campus policy, so it posed no problem to leave and catch a city bus.

Volkov gobbled up his breakfast and drove to the UW. After stopping and asking for directions, he found the main administration building. He parked two blocks away to keep anyone in the building from identifying the vehicle he drove, even though open parking spaces stood right out front. He walked into the building and approached the receptionist.

"Could I see the dean, please?" Volkov used care with his enunciation to avoid sounding Russian.

"Which dean? Academic Affairs, Student Affairs..."

"Yes, Student Affairs."

"That would be Dean Nielson. Do you have an appointment?"

"No, but it is urgent I see him."

"Who are you with?"

"The police. Officer Bergstrom."

"One moment." The receptionist picked up her phone and buzzed the dean's office. "I have a police officer, Bergstrom, who would like to see you right away." She hung up the phone and turned to Volkov. "You can have a seat over there. Someone will be right out to get you."

A moment later, Sally, Dean Nielson's secretary, emerged and brought Volkov to the dean's office, shutting the door behind him.

"Hello, I'm Don Nielson. What can I do for you, Officer Bergstrom?"

Volkov shook Nielson's hand. "Pleased to meet you, Mr. Nielson. I indicated to the receptionist that I am with the local police. Actually, I'm with Secret Service, but I didn't want to cause a ruckus." Volkov reached into his right breast pocket and pulled out his fake Secret Service I.D. "We have reason to believe that one of your students has information pertaining to matters of national security. All we have is his e-mail address." Volkov pulled a slip of paper from his pocket and handed it to the dean.

Nielson looked at the slip of paper, his forehead wrinkling. "encrypto@students.wisc.edu. Well, that certainly appears like an account here. Let me check." He picked up the phone and dialed the extension for the Computer Services Department. "Frank? Yes, this is Dean Nielson. I need you to get me the name of the person with the e-mail account encrypto@students.-wisc.edu. I need it immediately." The dean hung up the phone. "He'll call me right back. Well, I suppose you're from out of town."

"Yes, I am," Volkov replied. Nielson assumed he must be from Washington D.C., but decided not to pry. They sat uncomfortably for a few moments, and the phone rang.

"This is Dean Nielson. Yes." The dean picked up a pen. "Good." The dean started to write but abruptly stopped. "Oh. Okay, thank you. Good-bye." Nielson frowned and looked at Volkov. "Well, I have the name for you. The student is Kent Dalton. Actually, he's a former student. He was just expelled yesterday for inappropriate use of the computer system here. What has he done now?"

"I'm not at liberty to discuss details. Where can I find him?"

"He's a high school student, taking a couple classes here. He's rather advanced, academically. His father, John, is a professor of engineering here, chairman of the department."

"Where would Kent be now?"

"Well, I'm not sure. Possibly at high school. We can check with his father." Dean Nielson reached for the phone again.

Volkov raised his hand to stop him. "No, that won't be necessary. Given the sensitive nature of this matter, I don't want his father alerted until the situation is secured. We can't have extremely sensitive and vital information inadvertently destroyed or altered. Mr. Dalton will, of course, be notified once everything is under control. I'm sure you understand."

Nielson pulled his hand away from the phone and folded his hands on his desktop. "Of course."

"Would your registrar or admissions department have information which would assist me in locating Kent?"

"Actually, I can give you what you need. Their home phone number and address is right in the phone book. Let me see." He pulled a phone book from a desk drawer, flipped through the book and ran his finger down a page. "Here it is. 618 Oak Street. The phone number is 555-4968. If I remember correctly, Kent goes to school at Emerson High— that's on Garfield Avenue."

Volkov took notes on a pocket-sized notepad. "Thank you very much."

"Would you like me to do anything else?"

"No, that should be sufficient for me to locate him. Thank you for your cooperation." The men shook hands, and Volkov left the building.

CHAPTER TWENTY-NINE

Gene arrived at Denny's but walked right past at first to see if any government vehicles were around. He stopped outside the door and popped a Jolly Rancher in his mouth. When he entered the restaurant, the smell of bacon hit his nostrils. He looked around, slipped to the back, and entered an "Employees Only" door into the kitchen and cornered his cousin Elaine.

"Gene, you can't be back here!" Elaine insisted, glancing across the kitchen at the cook, who had his back turned.

"Quiet," he whispered. "This is important. I don't have time to explain. Don't say *anything* to *anyone*, okay?"

"What's the big deal?"

"You've got to believe me. My life is in danger, and so is Kent's. I'm meeting someone here in a few minutes. Have you seen anyone suspicious?"

"What do you mean your life is in danger?"

"I said I don't have time to explain. Have you seen anyone suspicious?"

"I don't know. There was a guy who sat down an hour ago but left before he ordered. Other than that, nothing but the usual freaks."

"What did he look like?"

"I don't know. He was black, tall, wearing a suit—that's all I remember. I just thought it odd the way he acted."

"Elaine, take this envelope. Don't open it. Call me at home tonight. If anything seems wrong, give this envelope to the cops. Whatever you do, don't read it. The police will know what to do with it."

"You're scaring me, Gene. What's going on? Are you dealing drugs?"

"I gotta get out there now—it's almost ten. I'm expecting a guy carrying a *Washington Post* in his right hand. He'll be in a suit—I don't know if he's black or not. If you see him before me, let me know."

Gene whirled and walked out of the kitchen to the front. Another waitress came over to seat him. "A booth please. I'm expecting someone else." He positioned himself by a window in the back corner where he could face the door.

Before the waitress had a chance to bring the menu, a black man entered the building wearing a long, charcoal gray wool overcoat and a navy blue, single-breasted suit. His right hand carried a folded newspaper. It appeared to be the *Washington Post*, but Gene couldn't read the name from across the room.

The man scanned the restaurant a few times. When his gaze returned to Gene's part of the room, Gene motioned with a single finger for him to come over. As he approached, Gene confirmed that he carried the *Washington Post*.

"Are you Paul Burrell?"

"Who are you?"

"Encryptomash."

"*You* are Encryptomash?"

"Yes. Well, sort of. I just kinda help out," Gene said, partly out of modesty, partly to avoid blame when the shit hit the fan. "So, are you Paul Burrell?"

"Yes. Why are we meeting here?"

"I feel safer here, that's all."

Elaine suddenly showed up with two menus. "Good morning, gentlemen. Can I get either of you coffee?"

"Yes," Burrell replied.

Elaine slowly walked away trying to catch any snippet of conversation she could.

"You better not have made me fly all the way from Virginia for some adolescent prank."

"This is no prank. I wish it were. Our lives really are at risk."

"Let me get this straight. You and your partners . . . who else is involved in this?"

"Just one other guy. I can't tell you who he is."

"Okay, you and your partner have been decoding secret messages for a guy named Nick who you think is in the Russian *mafiya*. Is that right so far?"

"Yeah."

"How do you know this guy is in the *mafiya*? You've just been dealing with him by computer, right?"

"The messages said he was *mafiya*."

"How do you know the messages aren't just baloney?"

"You've got to promise us immunity before I can tell you more."

"Immunity for what?"

"Uh, for anything we might have done wrong." Gene had almost blurted out that their engagement in illegal computer activities, but he realized the CIA probably knew nothing of this.

"I can't promise you immunity. Only a prosecutor can, and I don't even know if you've done anything illegal, except maybe jerking me around. Anyway, I don't see you have much choice other than to tell me what's going on. You said they're going to kill you. We can't protect you until you tell us what's happening."

"Okay, okay. They were paying us cash to decode the messages—wire transferred."

"How much cash?"

Elaine reappeared. "Here's your coffee. Are you ready to order?"

"I'll just have this, thanks," Burrell replied.

Gene looked at Elaine and scowled. "Nothing for me." She turned around, and Gene watched her silently as she walked away.

He looked at Burrell. "A thousand dollars for each message cracked." Gene lied, figuring that he and Kent probably owed taxes on the money. "We were supposed to get double that for each, but the messages appeared to be gibberish until we figured out they were supposed to be in a Russian font instead of the English characters we were seeing. We cracked the PGP encryption and then sent back the gibberish to Nick. Of course, he knew what to do to make it readable. Once we figured out it was Russian, we were able to translate it and learn what went on."

"What exactly is going on?"

"Well, it's kind of hard to piece it all together from a just a few messages, but it seems Nick intercepted secret Russian government communications relating to shipments of plutonium 239, highly enriched uranium and other materials which could be used to construct nuclear bombs. We think Nick intended to steal the shipments and sell the goods to Iran. We were worried, because they were definitely moving enough stuff to reach critical mass."

"Critical mass?"

"Yeah, you know—it takes a certain amount of uranium or plutonium to make a workable bomb."

"Isn't that quantity classified information?"

"Yeah, but everybody knows how much it takes to make a bomb—about 5 to 7 kilograms of P-239, a chunk about the size of a billiard ball. It takes roughly twice as much uranium."

Burrell's face started to lose some of its skepticism.

"Anyway," Gene continued, "it was clear the Russian government employee writing the messages knew he had a leak of information from his department, but he didn't suspect his encrypted messages. He thought secret information was getting to someone named Nikolai Volkov— we assume it's the same guy we've been dealing with."

"So how does all this relate to you and your fear for your lives?"

"When we got the last message translated, we put it all together. That message contained specifics on the dates, location, and mode of transportation. We felt we shouldn't give that information to Nick, so we sent him a fake message designed to throw him off the trail. Unfortunately, Nick figured out what we were doing."

"How did he find out?"

"We're not sure. We think either our message translation was flawed, or the message we created contradicted information he had from another source. He's threatened to kill us if we don't give him the real message by today at 3:00 a.m."

"Three in the morning?"

"Yeah, our deadline was nine in the morning, Greenwich Mean Time—that's the point from which all time zones in the world are calculated—Greenwich, England. We are six hours behind Greenwich. When you're e-mailing people around the world, it's common to use GMT as a standard. Here, I've got a copy of the last message we cracked and also a copy of Nick's threat."

Burrell studied the papers. "Well, this raises a lot of questions, and I need to check some other sources for answers. I'm going to take you with me down to the FBI office I'm working out of, so I can make some calls."

"There's something else you need to know. When your office wouldn't commit to getting someone here today, we got scared and sent the real message to Nick."

"You what!" Gene felt Burrell's eyes boring into him. "Let's go!" Burrell barked.

Gene rode in a rented Taurus to the FBI office, staring out the window the whole time to avoid looking at Burrell. Burrell continued to fire questions, probing every aspect of what Gene knew, testing his credibility about what appeared to be a far-fetched story.

The pair arrived at the FBI office, and Gene entered, feeling a hard lump in his throat. He was placed in an interrogation room and left to sit by himself. Burrell shut the door, and Gene watched through the partially closed blinds as he walked away.

Burrell went to an unused desk the FBI allowed him to use, picked up the handset of the phone, and quickly punched out a number. "Hi, Chuck, this is Paul. Yeah, I got one of 'em here. There's supposedly another one too. Have you checked on the 'product' transfer? I suspect you'll get a more favorable response when you give them the details I'm about to fax you. I have one of the intercepted messages, and it's pretty specific.

If it's authentic, the Russians will bite. Bad news, though—these two supposedly provided the intercepted message to the bad guys."

Timothy S. Jacobson

CHAPTER THIRTY

Volkov left the University and drove to a nearby pay phone, where he placed a call.

"Kirill, this is Nikolai. I have located him. He's just a boy. His name is Kent Dalton."

"Nikolai, our friend, Boris Levovich, in Minatom has reported that the U.S. State Department is inquiring about nuclear transfers. The boy must have contacted the authorities already."

"That does not surprise me. I am surprised the American government has taken it seriously enough to do something. Our government won't trust the Americans on this issue and won't tell them anything. I'll have to move quickly to get Mr. Dalton before the U.S. is successful in corroborating his story. Anything else?"

"We are set to go on a 'train ride' in just over an hour."

"I look forward to your report. Oh, and Kirill, while I expect this to be an easy job, as usual, if you don't hear back from me in twelve hours, I want you to see that the boy is taken out."

"Of course."

Volkov jumped into the Grand Am and peeled away. He arrived at Emerson within a few minutes, and drove around all sides of the school to familiarize himself with entrances to the building and the layout of the streets. Volkov parked out of sight, studying the school in greater detail as he walked toward it. He stepped in the front door and entered the main office.

"I'm Detective Jones from the Madison Police Department," Volkov said, flashing a badge. "I'm here to see a student, Kent Dalton. We believe he may be a witness to a crime, and we need to take him down to the station to see if he can provide us with any leads."

"One moment, please." The receptionist rose from her desk and walked back to the principal's office. "There's a police detective at the front desk wanting to take Kent Dalton to the station for questioning—says Kent may have been a witness to a crime."

"Page Kent to come to the office."

"Yes, sir." The receptionist walked back out to her desk. "Excuse me, Detective, I need to check Kent's class schedule to make sure he's here right now. Some days he's at the university. If he's here, I'll page him. Please have a seat while you're waiting."

The receptionist sat down and typed information into her computer. After a moment, she looked over at Volkov. "Yes, he should be here." She paged his classroom, requesting him to come to the office right away.

A minute later, Kent cautiously entered the office, expecting further trouble from his rampage on the computer the previous day.

"Oh, hi, Kent," the receptionist said. "This is Detective Jones from the police department. He has some questions for you."

The blood drained from Kent's face. Either he was in deep shit for what he'd done to Sam, or the police had figured out he blew up the dumpster. Perhaps, worse, his computer activities might have been tracked down more carefully, and his breach of thousands of computer systems discovered.

Volkov sprang from the chair. "Hi, Kent. I need to take you to the station to answer a few questions. We need help in an investigation we're conducting."

"Uh, yeah."

The pair walked outside and around the corner where Volkov had parked. The Russian said nothing, not wanting to tip Kent off as to his identity.

"This doesn't look like a cop car," Kent said as he stood by the passenger door.

"I'm a plainclothes detective. It's not supposed to look like a cop car. Get in."

Kent crawled in and fastened his seat belt. Volkov didn't bother with the seat belt. He started the car, and as he put the transmission in "drive," Kent noticed that the doors locked automatically.

After they had traveled what Volkov deemed a safe distance from the school, and sure no one followed them, the Russian's demeanor changed from a smiling police detective to cold and menacing. "Kent, you have something I want," he said, staring straight at Kent instead of at the road in front of him.

"What?"

"You have certain technology you've been using to play games with me."

A shiver ran through Kent's body. He gasped. His eyes widened as he realized he was about to die.

"Don't get any ideas—I don't want to have to shoot you," Volkov bluffed, since he didn't have a gun. Volkov didn't need a gun; killing was much cleaner when snapping someone's neck than blasting holes through him. Less messy and no chance for someone to be revived as a witness.

CHAPTER THIRTY-ONE

Burrell received the call from Chuck in Langley. "We've reviewed your fax. Russia won't confirm any of it, but we don't think it's fabricated—it's too consistent with what we know regarding locations, identities, and methods of transport. Not only that, but conditions in Russia are ripe for this kind of activity. There are extreme shortfalls in Russia's security and accounting systems for highly enriched uranium and plutonium—bomb grade materials. Russia still has a paper-accounting system that hasn't even kept track of some hidden caches of the stuff, which is used by Russian plant managers to make up shortfalls in meeting production quotas. There have already been four confirmed serious thefts, but fortunately none has reached sufficient quantities for making a bomb so far."

"Yeah, and if the information about the 'product' transfer is true, then the threats on these kids' lives must be true too. Keep me posted," Burrell said.

He trotted to the interrogation room where Gene waited. "Look, if you care about your friend, you better tell me where I can find him right away. We have a serious problem on our hands."

Gene stiffened with fear. "His name is Kent Dalton. He's a student at Emerson High School."

Burrell ran back to his desk and pulled out the phone book, then punched out the number for Emerson.

"Emerson High School, how may I direct your call?"

"Get me the principal—this is an emergency."

"I'm sorry. Principal Bailey stepped out a few minutes ago. Would you like to speak to the Assistant Principal Joan Wasserman?"

"Sure, anybody." Burrell tapped his pen down hard on the desk several times while he sat on hold.

"Hi, this is Joan Wasserman."

"This is Agent Paul Burrell from the Central Intelligence Agency. I understand you have a student named Kent Dalton. There may be a dangerous individual who will try to contact him at school. He or she may pose as a relative of Kent's, or as a law enforcement officer. Do not let Kent have contact with any strangers until we are able to arrive. If someone shows up asking to see Kent, act natural and stall them. We'll be there shortly. If you need to reach me, call the local FBI office."

"Okay. What was your name again?" Wasserman asked, not knowing Kent had already left.

"Paul Burrell."

"How will I know you are you and not the other person?"

"Good question. Keep Kent protected and we'll sort it out after we get there. Just so you recognize me, I'm a tall black guy with a charcoal-gray overcoat.

Burrell hung up and hurried over to Steve Krenz, head of the Madison FBI office. "We've got an emergency here, a kid from Emerson High School, Kent Dalton. There may be someone trying to kill him, a professional. If there is any law enforcement near the school, we need to get them there right away. I'm also going to need someone to ride with me, plus a backup car. Someone needs to check with the airport to see if anyone has flown in from Russia. I've already contacted the school.

Krenz got up from his desk, stepped out his door, and started barking orders. "Joe, you go with Paul here. Bill and Pete, you follow. We have a student at Emerson, Kent Dalton, whose life may be in danger. This is a professional killer we're talking about. John, you tie in with the city police and see if anyone is already out by there."

Burrell and company poured out the door.

Joan Wasserman buzzed the receptionist. "Alice, could you come in here right away?"

"Sure." She hurried into Wasserman's office.

"Alice, we have a problem. Someone might come looking for Kent Dalton. If anyone does, stall them and let me know right away."

"But Kent just left with a police detective a few minutes ago."

"Oh, my God. What happened?"

Alice shifted with uneasiness. "He said Kent may have witnessed a crime, and he needed to take him to the police station for questioning."

"What did he look like?"

"Short, thin, dark hair."

"Glasses?"

"No."

"Facial hair?"

"No, I don't think so," she said, shaking her head.

"What was he wearing?"

"A white dress shirt, dark blue tie."

"No uniform?"

"No, he was plainclothes."

Wasserman pulled out her phone book and looked up Federal Bureau of Investigation. She fumbled with the handset as she dialed the phone.

"Federal Bureau of Investigation, how may I direct your call?"

"Paul Burrell, please."

"One moment." The receptionist popped back on the line. "I'm sorry, we don't have a Paul Burrell here."

"He said he was a CIA agent working out of your office. It's about a Kent Dalton."

"One moment."

"This is Steve Krenz of the FBI. I understand you are looking for Paul Burrell?"

"Yes, this is Joan Wasserman, Assistant Principal at Emerson High. Mr. Burrell called and said we shouldn't release a student, Kent Dalton, to any strangers, but I learned that someone purporting to be a police detective took him for questioning just a short time ago."

"How long ago?"

"Apparently just a few minutes before Mr. Burrell called. I don't know, maybe five or ten minutes ago."

"What did this detective look like?"

"I didn't see him, but the receptionist said he had dark hair, a white dress shirt and a dark blue tie."

"What kind of car was he driving?"

"We don't know."

"Call me immediately if you get any more details."

"Certainly."

Krenz slammed the phone down. "Shit!" He put his hands over his face and dragged his fingers downward. "John, the kid's been taken by someone posing as a plainclothes cop. Call the department and make sure it wasn't a real one. Then I want an APB on this guy. All we know is he has dark hair, white shirt, and a dark blue tie, and he has a high school kid with him, Kent Dalton. Get a description from the other kid we got here. And find out where he lives and where they might go."

"Yes, sir," John replied, scurrying off.

The information got relayed to Paul Burrell that Kent had been taken from school. Patrol cars initiated a search pattern of possible routes Volkov might have taken leaving the school. Cars were quickly dispatched to the area around Kent's home and the university. Security was beefed up at the airport, and all major exits from the city were monitored.

Burrell now headed to Emerson High to obtain as much information as possible about Kent's abductor. He turned to his FBI driver and said, "You know, even with all these people looking, we hardly have a chance."

Timothy S. Jacobson

CHAPTER THIRTY-TWO

Volkov drove around the city looking for an out-of-the-way place to talk to Kent. He made Kent crouch down on the floor to throw off the police, and monitored police communications with a pocket scanner. He used an earphone so that Kent wouldn't know the police searched for them. After twenty minutes of driving, Volkov found a spot where he thought no one would disturb him, five blocks from where Kent and Gene had tested their explosive device. Volkov parked in an alley between two old, brick buildings.

"Put your hands on the dashboard," the Russian ordered.

Kent complied, and Volkov grabbed his left wrist to hold it tight against the dashboard while using his other hand to frisk.

"Empty your pockets—slowly," Volkov ordered.

Again, Kent did as told. A Swiss army knife and a comb emerged from one pocket, keys from another. Kent plucked a fat wallet from a back pocket.

Volkov grabbed the wallet from Kent's hand and opened it. He ignored the money, but pulled out numerous scraps of paper on which Kent had jotted notes and phone numbers.

He found a small sheet of stationary with the name "Samantha Trzebiatowski" printed in a flowing typeface on the top. Handwritten below were the words, "I'm going to get killed because of this computer program. Give me a call tonight after 7:00. 555-3287 Sam."

"Who is this 'Sam?'"

"She's a college student I know."

"She worked with you on the encryption program," Volkov said, not really asking.

"No, no. I tutor her in a computer class."

"That's not what it sounds like here."

Kent had forgotten about the note in his wallet and what it said. "Can I see that?"

Volkov handed it to him.

"This just means that she was going to flunk a certain programming assignment. It's not like it sounds. She doesn't know anything about the encryption program."

"Tell me about your method of deciphering messages."

"It's too hard to explain."

Volkov slapped Kent hard on the side of his head. "How stupid do you think I am? I'm not a programmer, but you can tell me in general terms."

"I just meant it would be easier to show you. We'll have to go to the university."

"You will have to tell me what's involved in the process first."

Paul Burrell and Joe Agger arrived at Emerson and met with Wasserman.

"Well, I'm not sure what to think about who's who here, but I called the FBI office, so I assume that's where you're from. I'm going to have you speak to one of our janitors. He saw Kent leave.

She walked Burrell and Agger into the main part of the school office and introduced them to the janitor, an older man.

"I was outside doing yard work when I saw them leave—a guy with dark hair and a tie, along with a kid. I thought it kinda odd they did not get in a car in one of the visitor parking spots by the front. No one seems to walk anymore if they don't have to."

"Did you see if they had a vehicle?"

"Yeah, when they went around the corner, I carried my rake to that side of the building and watched them get in a car."

"What did it look like?"

"Green, dark green. A sporty one."

"A sporty one, do you know what kind?"

The janitor hesitated. "I think it was one of those Pontiacs."

"How many doors?"

"Two."

"Anything else you noticed?"

"Nothing I can think of."

Burrell called Steve Krenz on his cell phone.

"Steve, this is Paul Burrell. He's driving a green Pontiac, two-door. I suspect he's monitoring communications. I'd advise that we give everyone the information without tipping off Nick."

"Understood. Anything else?"

"No. We're heading out to search."

Burrell hung up the phone, and he and Agger raced out of the school and hopped in the car.

"Where to?" Agger inquired.

"We've already got the house and university surrounded. Where else would they go?"

CHAPTER THIRTY-THREE

The White House

The President and Secretary of Defense William Morey entered the Cabinet Room where the Joint Chiefs of Staff had assembled, along with the Director of Central Intelligence, George McMillan. Conversation ceased as the group turned toward their Commander-in-Chief.

"Good morning, gentlemen," the President said, smiling and extending his hand. After the brief pleasantries, he instructed the Joint Chiefs and the DCI to sit at the rectangular table facing the windows while he and Secretary Morey seated themselves on the opposite side. He turned to Director McMillan. "George, I think you initiated this meeting. What's up?"

"Thank you, Mr. President. I'm going to be brief. We have information that the Russian *mafiya* may be in the process of intercepting a Russian train carrying a large quantity of bomb-grade plutonium, and that these actions may be taking place as we speak." McMillan swept his eyes about the room to gage the reaction. "We have been sending feelers through the State Department to the Russian government in an effort to confirm our information. The Russians aren't talking. In addition, we believe there are one or more terrorists in Madison, Wisconsin, attempting to acquire advanced encryption-breaking technology and/or to assassinate an American computer genius who apparently supplied the *mafiya* with technical assistance inadvertently."

The President squeezed his chin with his left forefinger and thumb. "If a train is being intercepted now, can we observe this by satellite?"

"The satellite images are being analyzed, and we have observed a train leaving the Lomonosov nuclear facility in southern Russia. Unfortunately, our satellite has moved out of position. It will be another thirty minutes or so before we can collect new images in the relevant area."

Commandant of the Marine Corps Fred Hallett wrinkled his brow as he looked at the DCI. "Why haven't I heard anything in my Defense Intelligence Agency briefings about an imminent theft?"

The CIA had been receiving plenty of criticism for failing to anticipate major events, such as India's testing of a nuclear bomb, and the Director looked indignant.

"We learned of this situation less than twenty hours ago," the DCI said. "We weren't able to confirm any of it until just this morning and, quite frankly, we are still speculating about much of it. But given the seriousness of the problem, we aren't taking any chances. The DIA didn't know about this situation because the CIA got contacted directly by an associate of the computer hacker."

The chairman of the Joint Chiefs cleared his throat. "Does your intelligence suggest what the *mafiya* intends to do with the plutonium if they obtain it?"

"It probably depends on the quantity. Undoubtedly, they'll try to sell some in the Middle East, probably Iran or Iraq. We believe they may have worked out deals in advance. The *mafiya* may also want to use some directly for terrorist activity. It could be used to strengthen a republic seeking to break away from Russia. . ." Director McMillan paused and looked directly at the President, ". . . or for blackmail by bringing a bomb to the U.S."

"Under any of those scenarios, great destabili-zation is likely," the Army Chief of Staff warned. "The U.S. could become the ultimate target of one terrorist group or another. If a large quantity of high-grade plutonium is stolen without a quick recovery, the risk of a nuclear explosion in a major U.S. city becomes a million times more likely. It wouldn't take the Iranians long to get a bomb over here either. Their nuclear experience with the Bushehr facility probably has enabled them to create all necessary components for the bomb other than a sufficient quantity of fissionable material. The White House could be ground zero in a week."

"What are your recommendations for action?" the President asked.

"We should offer military assistance to the Russians," the DCI answered, "either to prevent the theft, or recover the nuclear materiel if it's already been taken. As for the terrorists in Madison, the CIA is working cooperatively with the FBI and local authorities. I think it would be an overreaction to mobilize military forces in Wisconsin."

"The Russians aren't going to invite our military forces in," the Army Chief of Staff grumbled. "They'll be too damn suspicious. We can certainly offer to help, but a realistic goal would be to feed them our intelligence."

"I agree," the President responded. "But can our forces contain the movement of plutonium, keeping it within Russia's borders?"

"If everyone could turn their attention to the map in the briefing papers," Director McMillan instructed. "We believe the plutonium is being transported from the Lomonosov nuclear facility near Ordzhonikidze through a rugged stretch of the Caucasus Mountains on the route indicated in red, and then north toward Moscow. The interception is likely to take place somewhere in the mountains."

"If the *mafiya* succeeds in stealing the plutonium, how will they transport it?" the President asked.

"There are basically two ways," the Marine Corps commandant interjected. "Either by truck or by air. Land transportation is unlikely if they're smart. It would take too long, and they'd be vulnerable the entire time. Of course, air transport of plutonium is not safe from the standpoint of the civilian population, but I doubt the *mafiya* is concerned about public safety."

"Back to the President's earlier question about placement of our forces," the Chief of Naval Operations said, "it may be difficult to get Navy fighters from a carrier in the Persian Gulf to the part of Russia between the Black and Caspian Seas in the small window of time the plutonium would be airborne. On the other hand, the F-16's patrolling the northern no-fly zone of Iraq from the al-Kharj base in Saudi Arabia could respond more quickly. There is still going to be a significant time problem unless we know as soon as the plutonium is in the air."

Air Force Chief of Staff Clark Saunders leaned forward. "I agree. The Russians will be in a much better position to intercept, because they can put their planes in the air immediately, whereas we have to wait and then fly through hostile airspace. Not to say we shouldn't be prepared to do this anyway."

Secretary Morey spoke up. "I suggest we coordinate our air power in the region immediately: change our Iraqi flight paths to stay as far above the 36th Parallel as possible, put our carriers on alert and move them in, and get some AWACS so we can locate the *mafiya* aircraft. We'll keep the Russians informed, and leave a standing offer of direct assistance."

"Agreed," the President said. "Anything else?" He rose from his chair and turned to Secretary Morey. "You coordinate things. Keep me informed."

Moscow

Leonard Berezovsky, the sixty-one-year-old head of Russia's Federal Security Service (FSB), sat unblinking behind the heavy, dark wood desk, staring at Aleksandr Vid, his deputy, from bulldog eyes which bulged out from the baggy tissue of his face. Vid opened his mouth to speak, but Berezovsky cut him off, the words emerging with a measured pace. "Why do we have the U.S. State Department calling us about a plot by the *mafiya* to steal plutonium from *our* government? What is it the damn Americans know that we don't?"

Vid fidgeted with a pen. "Our agency has been following Volkov's activities. We just have not had enough solid evidence to do anything."

Berezovsky pounded his thick fist on the desk. "Slippery bastard!" The anger seemed to drain with this remark. "Well, we nailed his old man, and now he's going to get nailed too."

"Too bad Nikolai didn't learn from his father's mistakes."

"My guess is that he blames the government for Mikhail's early death. Well, I'm not convinced they have what it takes to touch one of the trains, but inform the person in charge of transport about what's going on, and step up security. I want immediate around-the-clock surveillance on all known associates of Volkov. I also have to believe there's a leak at Minatom. I want the word spread that Volkov's buyers are working for us. When the rumor is relayed to Volkov's people, we will have found the leak. I want arrests within forty-eight hours."

"Yes sir."

Madison

"How long have we been driving?" Joe Agger asked, as he sped down yet another city street.

"Burrell sighed. "I don't know. Ten minutes maybe. Too damn long."

Several minutes later, the dispatcher radioed for Agger, who in turn acknowledged.

"Two possible suspect vehicles. One parked illegally on East Washington near Ingersoll Street by the Octopus Car Wash. The other sighted going through a red light at Iron Bridge Road and Dayne Street, where it caused another vehicle to leave the road and hit a pole."

"Ten-four," Agger answered.

"Which one?" Burrell asked.

"I think I know which one is most likely," Agger responded, while accelerating.

Timothy S. Jacobson

CHAPTER THIRTY-FOUR

"The process?" Kent believed his exclusive knowledge of the encryption-breaking program and enormous computer network was the only thing keeping him alive, and now Volkov demanded he reveal the secret.

"I'm trying to think of where to start. Basically, I created a superior algorithm for quickly eliminating a large number of unlikely encryption keys for any given message. Then my program brute-forces its way through the possibilities remaining. Most programs treat the possibilities equally and waste a lot of time."

Volkov raised an eyebrow and nodded. "You obviously are not running this on a single machine. What kind of a networking setup do you use?"

"It runs on numerous machines simultaneously. The main control program is written in 'C' and runs under UNIX, but the distributed computing tasks run on multiple platforms, including Windows."

"How can we access the program from my laptop? I want to see it."

"We can't." Kent lied. "I built in a security feature so it can't be accessed remotely—we have to be physically present at the university on one of their terminals."

"That was not a smart thing to do, Kent. You had better think of a way we can get it without you and me going to the university. And if you can't. . ."

Kent had gradually moved his hand over to the door handle by the power lock button. He sensed the questions, and his life, were about to come to an end. He glanced over Volkov's shoulder as if he had seen something. Volkov jerked his head to look back. In that instant, Kent hit the unlock button and flung open the door. Volkov turned back to Kent and grabbed at him, catching the edge of Kent's tattered, unbuttoned flannel shirt. Kent thrust himself backward with his feet, pushing himself out the door. The momentum combined with Volkov's strong grip caused the shirt to rip and sent Kent spinning as he fell out the car door onto the pavement onto his right shoulder, his forehead and left hand scraping across the ground.

Kent jumped up, stumbled for an instant, and then ran behind the car and exited the alley, turning left, figuring it would be difficult for Volkov to shoot him through the back window of the car.

Volkov, who had the car running the whole time, popped it in reverse and punched the accelerator, leaving the passenger door open. The tires spun as the car hurtled backwards swaying from side to side as Volkov tried to steady it.

Kent ran down the sidewalk, his legs furiously pumping. Volkov flung the car out onto the street and hit the brakes, causing the passenger door to shut itself. He popped the shift lever into drive and floored it, again spinning the wheels. The car thrust forward, and Volkov drove it over the curb with a violent bump and up onto the sidewalk with two wheels, racing toward Kent.

Kent looked over his shoulder at the car bearing down on him, its engine roaring like a mad demon. He needed to clear the end of the building, but the car was almost upon him. He strained with every muscle to push himself faster. Blood spilled down from his forehead into his right eye, clouding his vision.

As Kent reached the end of the building, he turned the corner into another alley, the bumper of the car grazing his heel. The car shot past, and Volkov hit the brakes, skidding into a metal sign post on the sidewalk, knocking it over as it cut into the bumper and smashed the grill. Volkov whipped into reverse and backed up to the alley. Kent already had run half way through, and Volkov doubted he could get the car past a dumpster and some scrap metal piled there. He decided to catch Kent at the other end.

Kent continued to run as fast as he could, his lungs burning from his deep, gasping breaths. He noticed a fire escape ladder, and considered going up until he realized he would be an easy target for a gun. He continued on down the alley, not realizing Volkov had sped down and around to meet him there.

Upon reaching the other end of the building, Volkov turned left into the left lane, momentarily forgetting what lane to drive in. As he rounded the corner at high speed, he saw a car flying toward him from the other direction in the same lane, and he swerved, jumped up onto the sidewalk on the right side of the street, and struck a building with the corner of his bumper, slamming his head into the steering wheel.

Paul Burrell and Joe Agger leaped out of the other car and ran toward Volkov.

Kent emerged from the alley just as Agger's car shot by, and he stood watching as Volkov hit the building. As Burrell ran over to Volkov's car, Agger turned around and saw Kent. "Hey, kid, come here."

Kent turned around and ran back down the alley, not knowing for sure who these people were or how much trouble he might be in. Agger, with long legs and a thin, athletic build, sprinted after Kent. Near the other end of the alley, Kent, his vision still obscured by blood, tripped on some debris and fell, again tearing up his hands and scraping his knees. Agger quickly was upon him, grabbing the back of his shirt. Kent struggled for a moment, but then gave up, his aching body becoming like gelatin. Agger peeled him off the ground.

Burrell had his gun drawn, pointed at Volkov's head through the car window. Volkov, disoriented from the collision, sat for a moment with his head against the steering wheel. Burrell jerked the car door open, shouting, "Hands behind your head!" Volkov snapped out of his trance and complied. "Outta the car," Burrell barked. Volkov pivoted his body and eased his legs onto the ground. Slowly he stood up, facing Burrell, his eyes burning with contempt.

Burrell took a step back to keep himself out of range in case Volkov lunged at him. "Turn around and put your hands on top of the car." As soon as Volkov complied, Burrell stepped up and kicked his feet farther apart to keep him precariously balanced. He frisked Volkov thoroughly, then pulled one arm down to cuff, followed by the other arm.

A city squad car arrived; two officers got out and walked over to Burrell and Volkov.

"Hello, gentlemen. You missed the party, but you're just in time to help clean up. Could you do me a big favor and take this guy in? I've got to help look for a kid."

"Sure, no problem," one of the officers replied. "What you got him on?"

"Attempted murder, for starters. Write him up for driving on the wrong side of the road, while you're at it. Watch him closely, guys. He's a pro."

The other cop grabbed Volkov by the shoulder and turned him with a jerking motion. The cop opened the rear door of the squad car and pushed Volkov in. The three drove off.

Agger marched Kent back to the car. As they emerged from the alley, Burrell looked over their second catch of the day, paying particular attention to the blood oozing from several parts of Kent's body. "You must be Kent," he said, finally seeing the mastermind behind all this trouble. Kent nodded. "You had us a bit worried. Are you okay?"

"Yeah, I guess so," Kent assumed since he was standing up.

"Joe, I think we better wait here with Kent for an ambulance."

A couple sirens could be heard approaching. Burrell turned to Kent. "Well, Kent, it looks like we're going to need your testimony to put Nick away. I'm sure you'll want to help us, unless, of course, you don't mind Nick running free in your neighborhood."

Volkov was taken in, fingerprinted and photographed. Allowed a phone call, he used it to call Kardirov collect. "Kirill, I have been arrested in Madison."

"Oh, no."

"I want you to arrange for our friends in Chicago to come here and fix the problem. I also need you to find the best criminal lawyer around. Get someone local who knows the judges. I haven't had a bail hearing yet, but I'm sure it will take a lot of cash to get me out. Have it ready. Also, there's a Samantha Trzebiatowski who may be working with Kent. She's a college student. Find her."

Kardirov called Yuri in Chicago to arrange for a lawyer to meet with Volkov and to have Yuri travel to Madison to kill Kent, the witness who could keep Volkov behind bars. He also wanted Samantha located. She may be useful in several ways, Kardirov thought.

Yuri, in turn, called his lawyer in Chicago.

"Smith, O'Donnel and Smith," the receptionist answered cheerfully.

"This is Yuri. I need to talk to Frank right away."

"One moment, please."

"Yuri, what can I do for you?" Frank Smith asked when he got on the line a moment later.

"Frank, I got a friend in Madison who's been locked up. I need to get him the best local lawyer. Do you know any up there?"

"Sure, I know a few. Probably the best criminal lawyer there is a guy by the name of Maurer, Michael Maurer. That's

M-A-U-R-E-R. I went to law school with him. He used to be a prosecutor, then went into private practice five years ago. He does mostly white-collar criminal defense now. Give him a call and tell him I referred you."

"Thanks for the info."

"Sure. Good luck."

Yuri called Maurer and arranged for him to meet with Volkov. Then he and his brother Sergey drove their black Mustang GT to Madison.

Timothy S. Jacobson

CHAPTER THIRTY-FIVE

Republic of Georgia

"General, we're having problems making the final connection between the spur track and the switch," Lev reported. "With the short notice we received, we're a little understaffed."

"You've got ten fucking minutes until the train arrives," Potanin's voice crackled over the satellite-linked phone. "I want you to switch the train off the main line, even if you have to lay your men on the ground to close the gap. Is that clear?"

"Yes, sir."

Since the spur track had been laid toward the switch, instead of starting at the switch and working out, a gap had to be closed with a length of rail, and the measurements were slightly off, making the rail a hair too long.

"What are our options?" Lev asked.

"We don't have time to cut or grind it. Otherwise it would be easy to fix," a rail worker explained. "We've been banging on the track that's already been laid, but there's no room left to move it. The piece is only a couple millimeters too long, but with a thick piece of steel, we can't just squeeze it."

"She's gonna derail," a worker predicted.

Lev sighed, and turned away. He looked over at one of the helicopters and a cylinder of liquid nitrogen that would be used to cool the plutonium during transport. "I guess we won't need that anymore," he mumbled to himself. Then Lev cocked his head and whirled around to face the rail workers. "What if we cooled it with some of our liquid nitrogen? Would it contract enough?"

"It might," said one.

"Go get it," Lev shouted, and two of them sprinted toward the helicopter.

The men doused both the loose section of track and the part that had already been laid. White vapor rolled off the quickly-cooling steel, wrapped around the men's boots and formed vortexes as they moved their feet.

"How are we going to handle this thing?" one man asked, looking at his bare hands.

"Rip your shirt into two pieces and wrap it around your hands," Lev ordered.

They moved the piece of rail into position, but it still would not fit. "Keep pouring, and get it on all sides." Lev looked at his wrist. "We only have two minutes."

Lev radioed his tactical group in the woods to explain the current situation and to discuss how they would handle derailment.

The train could be heard straining up the steep grade below their level point.

Lev looked at his watch again even though the sound of the train now constituted a more reliable indicator of its impending arrival. "Try it again."

The men wiggled the rail and kicked at it, but it would not budge.

Lev looked over his shoulder. He saw the train through the bushes as it came over the crest, about 600 meters away.

The men struggled with their poor grip on the cold steel. They lifted both ends again to align it.

"Jam it in on the count of three," one man said. "One, two, three," he shouted through gritted teeth.

The track slid part way in. The men released their grip, but one had a sweaty finger that slipped off the cloth onto the frigid steel. He screamed as he yanked his hand off, leaving a large chunk of skin stuck to the rail. He backed away while another hit the rail with a sledge to drive it down. The rail secured, the men dived into the bushes.

The security forces from the General Staff on the train spotted the *mafiya* and began raking the ground with automatic gunfire. The engineer attempted to stop the train before it hit the switch, but the speed he had picked up upon hitting the level stretch propelled half the train onto the spur before it stopped.

Lev had wanted the whole length of the train to get onto the spur so it would be in better position for his forces. The engine itself, specially armored, with bulletproof glass, made it an impressive fortress.

Lev's men had to surrender much of their protective cover to attack the security forces in the middle of the train. Armor-piercing bullets crisscrossed the landscape. Gunfire sputtered from behind rocks and trees and out from slots in the box cars. Smoke grenades launched at the train provided cover as Lev's men advanced.

The first wave of *mafiya* soldiers ran toward the train swinging the muzzles of their guns back and forth as they fired. Bodies of several men were ripped open by the returning fire. Shrapnel flew from the bright flashes of several grenades exploding in close succession. Grenades could not be thrown at the train, because of the risk of damaging the nuclear containment units.

The engineer threw the train in reverse and began to back off the spur. Lev radioed for the second wave to descend on the train.

By now Lev's sharpshooters had located the openings through which the government forces fired. By precisely hitting these points, the sharpshooters provided some cover for the advancing *mafiya* forces.

One mercenary reached the train and grabbed onto a car, pulling himself up. As he ducked between two cars, he got shot, and dropped over the coupling between two boxcars.

Another mercenary jumped onto the same car, but held onto the underside while he looked for a way to stop the train. The government soldier who had shot the first mercenary on the train opened up a hatch on the end of the car, stepped out, and over the man on the coupling. He squatted and lowered his pistol to shoot the man clinging under the car.

The mercenary on the coupling regained some strength. He lifted his head and looked over his shoulder. He attempted to get up, but his legs failed to respond. He pulled his sidearm out of the holster and, body contorted, aimed by looking over his shoulder. The recoil knocked the gun from his weak grip, but the bullet accomplished its task. The government soldier fell onto the tracks.

The combatant under the car pulled himself up and applied the air brakes, stopping the train. The two adjacent cars were secured by the *mafiya*, and then the cars protected by underpaid and underfed soldiers were overwhelmed one-by-one.

Lev's men moved the train back on the spur and unloaded. Too much time passed unloading, and the train could not be returned to its previous course. They left it on the far end of the spur, invisible from the main line. Then they took up the portion of the spur near the switch so the spur track could not be seen by the next train that passed.

Lev's men prepared the plutonium for transport, and the two helicopters lifted off and headed south low over the trees. Lev returned to the satellite phone, first to General Potanin in Moscow, then to Ahmad in Iran to inform them the plutonium had been captured and was on its way.

Timothy S. Jacobson

CHAPTER THIRTY-SIX

Madison

Kent had been transported to University Hospital to be cleaned up and checked for injuries. The hospital notified John Dalton.

John raced to the hospital, arrived at the emergency ward, parked illegally, ran up to the desk and asked about his son. The nurse pointed to a room with a police officer stationed outside the door. As John approached, the officer held out his hand to stop him. "I'm sorry, sir, I need to see some identification."

"I'm Kent's father." John tried to walk past the officer, who stepped sideways to block his path.

"This room has been secured by order of the FBI. You will have to show me identification, or you'll be escorted out of the hospital."

"FBI? What the hell does the FBI have to do with this?"

"Do you have identification or not?"

John sighed and dug in his back pocket for his wallet. He pulled out his driver's license and handed it to the cop. "Okay, you can go in," he said.

Kent lay on the bed with large bandages on his forehead and hands, and one of his eyes had swollen shut. John sucked in a breath, put a hand to his mouth, and froze. "Kent, are you alright?"

"Yeah, Dad, I'm okay. I just got some bumps and bruises."

"What happened?"

"The Russian *mafiya* tried to kill me."

"The *mafiya*?"

"It's a long story. You know about the guy who figured out how to crack public key encryption?"

"Yes. What does that have to do with anything?"

"Well, that's me. I'm Encryptomash. After I posted on the Internet that I could crack PGP, I received some offers to do it for money. I did a few, and later figured out I dealt with the Russian *mafiya*. They were intercepting Russian government messages about the transfer of enriched nuclear materials they planned to steal and sell to Iran. To stop them, I sent a fake message. They got pissed when they found out, so they tried to kill me."

John put a hand on his forehead. "Why didn't you tell me?"

"I don't know. I. . ." Kent turned away.

"Excuse me, how's our patient doing?" a young doctor asked as he entered the room.

Kent turned his head to face the door. "I'm okay."

"Is the pain any better now?"

Kent wiggled his fingers and pointed toward his head. "I can't feel a thing unless I bump my forehead."

"You must be Mr. Dalton," the doctor said to John.

"Yes, John Dalton. Is he okay?"

"Well, he hit his head pretty good. We put in a few stitches. So far there's no sign of concussion. You'll need to watch him carefully for the next twenty-four hours. Check his eyes at least once an hour to make sure the pupils respond to changes in light. Ask him questions to make sure he's oriented as to time and place. You should wake him during the night to check him. If you notice anything unusual, call us immediately."

"I'll do that."

"Are you ready to go home, Kent?" the doctor asked.

"I guess so." Kent sat up slowly, then stood up, and John took his arm and walked him to the door.

The cop stopped them. "I have to take you down to the FBI office," he said to Kent. "Mr. Dalton, why don't you follow in your own car."

"Can't Kent ride with me?"

"I'm sorry. Your son is a witness to matters of national security. I have full responsibility for him, and I've been directed to take him to the FBI as soon as he's able to leave the hospital."

Burrell sat in a small office at the FBI building with the door shut talking to Vernon Coles, his boss in Langley. "We've apprehended a suspected member of the Russian *mafiya*—Nick Volkov. He's not talking, but we got two 'Encryptomash' kids—they're high school students. One's in the hospital right now, but once he's cleaned up, he'll be brought in here,"

Burrell said.

"Good. Will you have any trouble getting the kids to talk?"

"I don't think so. One told us a bundle already, but I think the other ran the show. They're not clean on this, so maybe we can get them to talk as part of a package."

"Be careful. Go by the book. I don't want to lose on a technicality."

"One of them—Gene—already mentioned immunity."

"Obviously, the FBI has jurisdiction in any criminal investigation of the boys, but you can stay involved to collect information as it pertains to ongoing national security issues. Let's make sure we get our priorities straight. First, we need testimony to put away Volkov. If we nail him, maybe we can use him to get others. Second, timing is critical right now—we need the kids to cooperate to bring out other *mafiya* members who are sure to follow."

"I don't think that's such a good idea. We're dealing with pros here, and these are just a couple of small town boys."

"Look, if we don't trap the bastards now, they're going to hunt down the kids, and continue to promote nuclear terrorism."

"I know. It's just. . ."

"The third priority is obtaining the encryption technology. Denise has briefed me on that issue. She believes the kids must have access to a large number of computers, and their access probably wasn't legal. Even a supercomputer couldn't do it alone so quickly. You have to find out how they succeeded."

CHAPTER THIRTY-SEVEN

Kathy Fisher, Gene's mother, tossed in her bed. Regardless of how long she worked the night shift at the factory, she could never adjust to sleeping during the day.

The phone rang, and she grabbed her husband's pillow to cover her head to muffle the sound. At last the ringing stopped.

She removed the pillow from her head and tried peaceful thoughts to relax. The phone started ringing again. By the time it rang a dozen times, Kathy dragged herself out of bed, swearing under her breath. As she picked up the handset, she shut her eyes and, with a dry mouth, whispered a raspy "Hello."

"Is this Kathy Fisher?"

It must be a salesperson, she thought. "Yeah, who's this?" A wrong answer and Kathy would hang up.

"Paul Burrell. I'm with the Central Intelligence Agency."

"The what?"

"The CIA."

Kathy's eyes were no longer closed. "Is this some sort of prank? If it is, I'm in no mood. . ."

"It's not a prank, ma'am. I'm calling about your son Gene."

"What about Gene—is he alright?"

"He's fine. He's with us at the local FBI office. We need you and your husband to come here and answer a few questions."

Kathy called Bud, Gene's stepfather, at work. She explained that Gene was at the FBI office and they had to go there to answer questions.

"What did your son do now?" Bud asked.

"My son? Don't give me that crap. You're responsible for what goes on in our house as much as anyone. If you were standing here, I'd slug you."

Bud decided to drop the argument. "Sorry. What do we need to do?"

"You need to leave work right away and pick me up. Then we'll drive to the FBI office and find out what's going on."

"Shit. How do I explain this one to the boss?"

"You'll think of something."

"Do we need a lawyer?"

"We can't afford a lawyer."

"I'll get there as quick as I can."

Kathy hung up the phone, then realized she needed to get dressed and brush her hair.

Burrell met with Kent while an FBI agent questioned Gene. The boys' parents sat in separate rooms for questioning about their level of knowledge of what had occurred.

Kathy and Bud sat on small, metal chairs right up against each other in a cramped interrogation room.

After several minutes, a man in an olive-drab suit entered the room. "I'm Agent Pete Stonedahl. Can I get you some coffee?"

"No thanks," Bud replied.

Agent Stonedahl looked at Kathy. She shook her head.

"Do you know why you're here?"

"No," Kathy answered.

"Your son, Gene, has apparently gotten mixed up with the Russian *mafiya*."

"What?" Kathy said. "How could he get mixed up with Russians? He never leaves Wisconsin."

"He's done it with computers," Stonedahl explained. "Apparently he and another boy were communicating with the Russian *mafiya* by e-mail. Do you know anything about this?"

Bud squirmed in his chair. "What are you talking about? Gene didn't have a computer until recently. It must have been that Dalton boy."

"Why do you say that?"

"Everyone knows Kent is some sort of computer whiz."

"And he's been in trouble lately, too," Kathy added. "Gene may not be the best student in the world, but he stays out of trouble. If he's not at home tinkering in the garage or watching TV, he's usually at Kent's house, or at the university with Kent."

"I didn't say your son has intentionally done anything wrong. We're just trying to figure out what's going on so we can stop the *mafiya*. We need your help. You say Gene goes over to the university with Kent. What do they do there?"

"To be honest, I really don't know," Kathy replied. "Kent's dad teaches over there, and he has a lab. I always thought it was good for Gene to spend time there, even though a lot of the students seem weird. We want Gene to attend college—we never had the chance."

"I heard Gene mention some sort of computer hookup to the brain," Bud said. "I don't know how that could involve the Russians, though. What's this about Russians, anyway?"

"It's still under investigation. Have you heard Gene on any unusual phone calls, or have you seen him talking to anyone out of the ordinary?"

Both Bud and Kathy shook their heads.

"Has Gene made any unusual purchases, or had more money than usual?"

"He's bought more music lately, and a used computer a while back," Kathy volunteered. "I told him to watch his spending."

"Does he have a job?"

"Lawn mowing in the summer, snow shoveling in the winter," Bud said.

"Would his odd jobs cover the purchases?"

Bud looked over at the wall as if the answer might be written there. "I don't know. I'm not sure how much he's earned or saved. He doesn't blow a lot of money on expensive shoes and stuff."

"I appreciate your cooperation," Stonedahl said. "I'll give you and Gene an escort home, and we'll provide twenty-four hour surveillance to make sure you're alright."

"Twenty-four hour surveillance? Why do we need that? Is someone after Gene?" Kathy asked.

"Not that we know of. We just want to be on the safe side."

When Stonedahl left the room, Kathy turned to Bud. "I'm really scared."

"I'm sure we'll be fine. They're giving us 'round-the-clock protection. You can't beat that."

Burrell started to speak, but Kent interrupted him. "You have to do something about Samantha Trzebiatowski. The *mafiya* thinks she's involved, and she's not."

"Who?"

"Samantha Trzebiatowski. She's a student at the University. Nick found a note in my wallet from her where she said she would get killed over a computer program. She was talking about a homework assignment, but I think Nick doesn't believe me."

Burrell ripped a sheet of paper from a legal pad and slid it to Kent with a pen. "Okay, write down her name, address, and phone number. Someone will take care of it. Now, what was really going on? I get the feeling from talking to Gene that you were calling the shots."

"It was the *mafiya* calling the shots."

"No, I mean between you and Gene."

"Yeah, I guess so."

"How did all this start?"

"I was working on kind of an artificial intelligence project at UW..."

"The university here?"

Kent looked down at the floor. "Yeah. I decided the best way to test the computing power of the system was to crack encrypted messages. I improved upon the algorithms used by others, and my system worked really well."

"Okay, then what?"

"I posted something on the Internet, to let others know it could be done, and shortly after that, Nick contacted me and asked me to crack messages. I didn't know he was with a criminal organization."

"And you did decode messages for them."

"A few."

"And at some point you figured out it was the *mafiya* sending the messages."

"Yeah, the *mafiya* was sending the messages to me. But the Russian government sent the messages originally. I assume Nick's people intercepted them."

"Have you ever seen Nick before today?"

"No."

"He picked you up from school today?"

"Yes."

"Why did you go with him?"

"The school receptionist called me to the office and said a police officer had some questions for me."

"What did you think he wanted to talk about?"

"I dunno. He talked about an investigation. He never said what about."

"Anything in particular you thought it might be about?"

Kent's heart sped up as he thought about the dumpster, having changed Sam's grades, and gaining illegal access to thousands of computers. "Well, I had just gotten in trouble at

UW for violating their computer policy. I thought it had something to do with that."

"What was that about?"

Kent hesitated and picked at his left thumbnail. "I kinda pulled a prank on a girl."

"I see. What did Nick say to you when he took you for a ride?"

"He wanted the secret to my technology."

"Did he threaten you?"

"Yeah, he threatened to shoot me. He also hit me alongside the head with his hand. And then he tried to run me over right before you guys got there."

"How did you get out of the car?"

"I distracted him, popped the power lock, and jumped out. We were parked then."

"You could have been killed."

"I thought I'd be killed anyway."

"Tell me about the technology you used to crack the messages."

"It's just a computer program."

"We know about your access to the computer systems," Burrell bluffed, "and we've spoken to Gene already, you know."

Kent bit his lip. They have me, he thought. "Yeah, I broke into them to get more computing muscle."

"You gained access to computers illegally?"

"I guess so."

Kent explained to a shocked Burrell that he had broken into *thousands* of computers. Burrell wrote out a statement summarizing what Kent told him, and obtained his signature.

He felt he had the leverage now to get the boys' cooperation. The *mafiya* would come looking for them, and they could be used to snare the *mafiya*.

Burrell walked over to the room where John Dalton waited. "You must be Professor Dalton."

"Yes."

"I'm Paul Burrell. I'm with the Central Intelligence Agency. Your son's friend, Gene, contacted my office yesterday. A lot has happened since then."

"Yes. And apparently a lot before that I didn't know about. If only Kent had come to me, this whole situation might have been avoided."

"This is very serious," Burrell said. "Not only do we have a problem with the *mafiya*, but also your son has informed me that he gained illegal access to thousands of computers to break encryption."

"He *what?*"

"He said it was some sort of worm program that would establish accounts on all sorts of university, government, and corporate computer systems. He would draw on the power of all those systems simultaneously."

John sat there dumbfounded.

"As I'm sure you know, Kent's activities comprise serious crimes. He could do some major time. Each computer he accessed is a separate crime. He could face life in prison and astronomical fines. I'm sure it wouldn't be good for your career either." Burrell paused for emphasis. "But I think we can work something out."

"Kent will testify against the *mafiya*. We will cooperate fully."

"That's good. I feel confident we can work together. I'm sure you don't want these dangerous people on the loose. I assume you realize there will be others looking for Kent. He's tried to keep them from obtaining the nukes they want to sell, and now he's caused one of them to be arrested."

"What else can we do?"

"We suspect there are other *mafiya* members in Madison as we speak, and if not, they'll probably arrive within the next twenty-four hours. We need your full cooperation to catch Nick's companions."

"We'll do anything we can to help."

Gene went home with his stunned parents. As promised, an FBI agent escorted them and stationed himself near their house to keep a twenty-four hour watch.

More careful precautions were taken for Daltons, since the *mafiya* knew their identity and where they could be found. Burrell obtained permission from John to tap his phone. FBI agents were stationed in four locations around the Dalton house, including in a van with electronic monitoring equipment. Burrell located himself in the van with an FBI agent driver, and the Daltons were instructed to keep their curtains tightly drawn and to stay away from windows.

Timothy S. Jacobson

CHAPTER THIRTY-EIGHT

Moscow

"Excuse me, sir, but there's a lieutenant from the Twelfth Department of the General Staff on the phone. He insists on speaking to you directly," Natasha said to her boss, Yevgeny Rohklin, Russia's Defense Minister. "He says it's an urgent matter of national security."

"How much vodka has he consumed?"

"He sounded sober, but out of breath. He's calling through a satellite link."

Rohklin scowled. "Put him through."

"This better be good," Rohklin said when he picked up the phone.

"Lieutenant Komandin, sir. I apologize for not following the chain of command, but a large quantity of bomb-grade plutonium has just been stolen, and I believe several former military officers are involved."

"Where and how?"

Komandin paused to catch his breath. "I'm assigned to the nuclear transport trains from Ordzhonikidze. We were put on alert by the FSB that the *mafiya* might try to intercept our shipment. When our communications went dead, my commanding officer had me jump off at the crest of a hill with a satellite phone to monitor the situation from a distance, and to attempt to reestablish communications. The *mafiya* managed to switch my train off onto a spur track, and they eventually gained control. I saw them remove the plutonium and transport it with two Mi-8 choppers. They were headed south to southeast."

"Thank you, lieutenant. We'll take care of this, and we'll send a rescue crew to help you out."

Rohklin called Leonard Berezovsky, head of Russia's Federal Security Service. When Berezovsky came on the line, Rohklin didn't bother with a greeting. "I just received a report that one of our nuclear transport trains from Ordzhonikidze has been captured by the *mafiya*. I was told that your department had advance notice of the attack. Why was I not informed?"

"It happened?" Berezovsky said with evident surprise. "Where's the plutonium?"

"On helicopters heading out of the country. Why was I not informed?"

"The U.S. State Department said they believed the *mafiya* may be plotting to intercept a train. That's not a new idea. I sent word to the train so our security forces wouldn't be caught off guard in case the Americans were right."

"Well, they were. Is there anything else I should know?"

"It sounds like you know more than I do."

"We're going to have to commence a recovery operation immediately. Make arrangements with your forces, and coordinate with the other services. I'm going to inform President Primakov of these developments."

Rohklin had Natasha get President Primakov on the line. While waiting to be connected, Rohklin lit a cigar. The ash had time to grow a bit before Primakov came on.

"Mr. President. I hate to call you with bad news, but the *mafiya* captured a nuclear transport train coming out of Ordzhonikidze. The plutonium is being carried south by helicopter. It's probably destined for Iran. I have initiated a recovery operation."

"How long before the criminals are stopped?"

"Their exact location has not yet been pinpointed, but given their departure time and direction of travel, we should be able to intercept within the hour. It will likely be near the Iranian border."

"Have the Iranians been contacted?"

"No, Mr. President."

"I assume you're not going to just shoot these choppers out of the sky when they're carrying plutonium. You'll need Iran's cooperation to capture them on the ground."

"Yes, I agree."

"Make contact with Iran, and then we'll convene a meeting with the FSB and the General Staff."

The White House

Defense Secretary Morey entered the Oval Office where the President sat behind his desk talking about budget issues with two legislative strategists. The President told the two he would finish the budget conversation later. They nodded, got up, and whisked past Morey out the door, shutting it behind themselves.

"Judging from your face," the President said, "I assume you have bad news."

"Our satellite images show a train from Ordzhonikidze has been stopped in the Caucasus, and it's positioned off the track. The Russian government could not deny that, but it won't confirm anything else. They want us to stay out of this."

"Those damn Russians!" The President glanced at his phone with a direct line to the Kremlin. "I should call Primakov and bitch him out. It was one thing to play secrecy games back when they had some internal controls, and the morale of their military wasn't so bad. But now that their pilots are being paid with vodka, they shouldn't be above asking for help."

"We have F-16's flying in circles on the northern border of Iraq, ready to move in if necessary."

"Should we ignore the Russians and send our planes in?" the President asked.

"It could be a bloody mess. Our AWACS plane has detected fighters moving south from Russia, and north from Iran, but we haven't picked up any transport-type aircraft yet. If they're helicopters, they might be flying too low to detect with the mountains in the way."

"What do you think the intentions of the Iranian fighters are?"

"I'm convinced the Iranian government is involved, and they've sent their pilots to ensure the plutonium gets to its destination."

"Where will the Russians intercept the Iranian planes?"

"Near the border between Iran and Armenia, although it looks like the Iranians will reach there before the Russians."

"Can we get our planes there first?"

"If we give the order now, our planes will arrive just after the other two sides. But if we send them, we risk war with two countries. Even if Russia and Iran don't overreact, if our planes go down, it could be like the botched hostage rescue in Tehran."

The President folded his arms and stewed over this dilemma, the frustration evident in his expression. "I can't just do nothing. I'm calling Primakov, and I'm gonna rip him a new asshole."

Madison

Due to the limited number of available FBI personnel, Steve Krenz enlisted local law enforcement to provide safety for Samantha Trzebiatowski. A twenty-two year veteran of the force, Mark Pielhop, was assigned the task. Pielhop, as fit as many new recruits, prided himself on receiving special assignments. He had seen plenty of bizarre activities, arrested numerous violent criminals, but had never faced professional hit men in Madison.

Officer Pielhop attempted to call Sam's dorm room from his desk, but got no answer. Her parents' number in Massachusetts yielded the same result.

Pielhop drove to her dorm. He parked in the university lot next to the building, and walked inside. He pounded on Sam's door and called her name, stumbling over "Trzebiatowski." No response.

He heard muffled voices coming from another room, and banged on that door. It opened a crack, and a cute young woman with brown hair and brown eyes peered out.

"Yeah?"

"I'm looking for Sam Trzebiatowski. Do you know who she is?"

"Yeah, she lives down the hall."

"Have you seen her today?"

"Around mid-morning, but not since then. Why?"

"It's important that I speak to her. If you happen to see her, could you ask her to give me a call?"

"Sure."

Pielop jotted his name and number on a page in a small notepad, ripped it out, and handed it to her. "If I'm not there when she calls, she should identify herself and ask for Captain Delaney. She should call, no matter the time of day or night. Also, if you see anyone suspicious around here, please give me a call right away."

Pielhop thanked her and walked away. He questioned other students about where Sam might be. No one had seen her or her roommate for several hours.

Pielhop returned to his car and radioed in the results of his search. Campus security was notified, and asked to contact the police if Sam could be located. Pielhop waited in his car and watched.

Over Armenia

Three MiG-29 fighters hurtled toward the Iranian border. A half-dozen Ka-50 Black Shark attack helicopters were also deployed to take over once the Mi-8's were forced to the ground, but they already lagged more than 200 kilometers behind the MiG's, and that gap grew by the second.

"Hunter One, our bird dog up above has sniffed out their heat trails." The radios crackled in the MiG's. "Adjust course seventeen degrees west."

"Adjusting course now. We do not have radar confirmation."

"They should be on the other side of the peak you're approaching. You should intercept in five minutes."

Flying low, the MiG pilots sweated as they increased their altitude to clear the mountain peak, wondering what they would discover on the other side.

The MiG's dropped down over the far side of the peak, hugging the contours of the earth. Their radar displays began to beep multiple times.

"Lodge Leader, we have. . ." the pilot paused to check the display again, ". . .seven birds flushed. I repeat, *seven* birds. Five of them are MiG's."

"Confirm assistance from the southern neighbor."

The lead Russian MiG pilot attempted to establish radio contact with the Iranian-owned MiG's which were screaming toward the Russians.

"Disengage, please," came the response in halting Russian. "We will take it from here."

"We appreciate the assistance," the Russian pilot responded, "but we have our orders to see the two choppers to the ground."

"The helicopters are now passing into our territory. We cannot authorize you to go further."

"We're going further with or without your authorization."

An Iranian plane squeezed off several rounds of machine gun ammunition near the Russian fighters as a warning, and tracer bullets painted luminescent arcs across the dark sky.

Undeterred, the Russian pilots swooped in closer. As the tones of radar locking sounded, an air-to-air missile streaked first from one and then from a second MiG.

The Iranians returned fire, and in an instant, a jumble of planes and projectiles, moved like a swarm of insects intent upon destroying one another. One of the outnumbered Russian planes got raked with machine gun fire before plunging down and away from its attacker.

Another Russian pilot gained a solid lock on an Iranian plane and fired. The Iranian pilot looked on in horror as the missile connected. The Russian pulled up as the bright flash hurtled fragments of the jet in all directions. A second Iranian plane exploded a moment later. The three remaining Iranian fighters disengaged and headed toward their base.

The fighter pilots resumed pursuit of the two helicopters. Without the protection of the Iranian fighters, the choppers put up little resistance to being herded north.

Timothy S. Jacobson

CHAPTER THIRTY-NINE

Madison

In the living room of their home, John demanded a full explanation from Kent. He fired question after question at his son, gave him a long talk, more of a fire-and-brimstone sermon than a lecture.

At 6:53 p.m., the phone rang. Kent sprang from the chair, paused while the phone rang a second time, then cautiously picked it up as if it were venomous if held wrong. "Hello?"

A gruff voice asked, "Is this Kent?"

"Yes."

"Is anyone else there listening?"

"No. It's just me." Kent's father stood a foot away straining to hear the conversation.

"Good. Keep very quiet. I would like to give you something to forget all about what happened today. Are you interested?"

"What do you mean?"

"How about that $100,000 you wanted?"

"Yeah?"

"Can you sneak out around midnight?"

"I . . . I think so."

"Meet me at Cedar Park, up on top of the hill by the big sculpture. Don't bring anyone with you, and don't contact the cops or you'll regret it."

"I won't."

The phone went dead.

"Who was that?" John asked anxiously.

"The *mafiya*, I assume. They want to meet me in Cedar Park at midnight."

"Well, that isn't going to happen. The FBI should be contacting us shortly. I'm sure glad they tapped the phone. Maybe they'll trace the call and catch them."

Burrell had indeed listened through headphones. He radioed the office. "Did you trace that call?"

"Yeah, I think we have a lock on it," Krenz replied. "Give me a minute."

Burrell shifted in his seat and looked over the electronic equipment while he waited.

"We got it. It's a payphone on the other side of town in a quiet neighborhood. We have someone heading there right now."

Yuri had hung up the payphone with his gloved left hand, leaving no fingerprints behind. He strolled around the corner to the waiting car and was gone in the four minutes it took to get a city cop there.

Krenz radioed Burrell. "He's gone."

"Damn it!" Burrell swore. "I'll call the kid and we'll play along with the caller."

"I hope you know what you're doing," Krenz cautioned.

Burrell was angry now, angry the caller got away, angry his boss in Langley had pressured him to use Kent as bait, and angry that this FBI S.O.B. questioned his judgment. "I know what the hell I'm doing. I didn't take this job yesterday."

The somewhat older Krenz knew when to take a step back to avoid a wasteful confrontation. "Hey, I didn't say you did. I'm a little concerned about the kid."

"Yeah, well, let's get a tactical team in there and seal it up airtight."

Burrell called the Daltons. Kent answered the phone.

"This is Agent Burrell. We traced the call, but they were gone when we reached the phone booth. I want to ask a favor. Shortly before midnight we'd like you to take your bike to Cedar Park. Do you know where it is?"

"Yeah, up on the hill."

"Good. You'll need to wear the bulletproof vest we provided, and also the wire so we can monitor anything you or anyone around you says. You'll have an earphone so we can talk to you. We'll have the park surrounded by sharpshooters with night vision equipment. If anyone approaching appears hostile or displays a weapon, we'll take him out. Can we count on you to do this?"

"Well, I don't think my dad will let me."

"Can you put him on the phone?"

"Agent Burrell wants to talk to you," Kent said, handing the phone to John.

"This is John Dalton."

"Hello, Professor Dalton. This is Agent Burrell. We traced the call to a phone booth, but they were gone before we arrived. I have just asked your son if he is willing to ride his bike up to Cedar Park to lure out the *mafiya*. I want to assure you we will have the park completely surrounded by sharpshooters with night vision equipment, and your son would be wearing a bulletproof vest. Obviously, since he's still a minor, we need your authorization."

"Absolutely not. I'm not going to allow my son to be bait."

"I understand your concerns, Professor Dalton. The problem is, if we don't flush these guys out now, they'll pursue your son until they've killed him. We want to end this as soon as possible, and while we have control of the situation, so your life can return to normal. Your cooperation will also help Kent with any charges resulting from his unlawful use of computers."

"Isn't there some other way you can do this? Why don't you send a cop there to pretend he's Kent?"

"Our concern is that they're watching your house now. The person who goes to the park has to come from your house. They may monitor Kent the whole way, and if we send someone else, they'll know he's an imposter and not show up."

"I believe it's a bad idea, and if you can think of anything else between now and midnight, please do. If you can't, however, Kent can go, but you have to promise to keep him completely protected the whole time."

"You have my promise. We'll keep him safe."

"You better." John looked at his son who mouthed the word "Sam." "Oh, I almost forgot. Kent wanted me to ask you if Sam Trzebiatowski is safe."

"Last I heard, she had been away from her dorm and hadn't been located.

Moscow

Boris Levovich looked across the expansive room cut up with cubicle walls. Two men in the opposite corner talked and laughed, but Boris couldn't hear over the steady hum of the building's ventilation system. He saw three women sitting at desks: one leafing through a stack of papers, one on the phone, and one pounding out words on a manual typewriter.

He ran his hand across his brow as he lowered himself into the chair. He picked up the handset of the phone, his hand tremoring as he dialed a number.

Kardirov answered.

"This is Boris. I'm sorry to bother you."

"Where are you?"

"At the office. I. . ."

"I thought you weren't allowed to make *personal* calls during work hours," Kardirov interrupted, angry that Boris' call might be traced.

"I need to speak to you right away. Can we meet?"

"This is not such a good time. I'm rather busy. Can't this wait?"

"No."

"Let's meet for lunch tomorrow," Kardirov responded, using the code phrase they had worked out to indicate a meeting that same day.

The young Russian agent rushed to a phone and called Aleksandr Vid. "We confirmed a leak. A call placed from Minatom right to Kirill Kardirov."

Vid smiled. "Good work. Who is it?

"We have a bit of a problem in that regard. The call was placed from the desk of an absent employee. The caller identified himself only as Boris—we don't know if that's his real name, or an alias. If it's real, there are a lot of employees with the name Boris. We're working to narrow it down, and we have some time—they're not meeting until lunch tomorrow. I just wanted to let you know about this right away, as you instructed."

"Any details on the conversation?"

"Not much. Boris claimed it urgent that they meet. Kardirov said it wasn't a good time but agreed to meet anyway."

"Have there been any problems keeping track of Kardirov?"

"He has tight security and the best technology for countering our surveillance. I have to believe he knows his phone is tapped."

"You're probably right, but he doesn't know we're monitoring calls originating from Minatom. I suspect their message was coded, and that he's not going to be concerned with our listening in. Just make sure you stay on him."

CHAPTER FORTY

Madison

At 11:45, Kent entered the garage, got his bike, and rode nervously toward Cedar Park, arriving two minutes before midnight. Sharpshooters had been surrounding the park for hours, monitoring any movement. No one had been detected in the park since about 10:30 when a pair of joggers went through. The FBI got concerned the *mafiya* became spooked and would not show. Burrell continued to reassure Kent they were watching him and that no one had been sighted nearby.

Kent walked up near the sculpture and sat on a park bench. He shook, continuously scanning the area around him looking for movement. Inky shadows from numerous trees danced rapidly across the park as the wind increased. Leaves crunched behind him. He gasped loudly as he whipped his head around.

"What?" asked Burrell through his earphone.

Kent peered into the darkness, but didn't see anything. Then he noticed a raccoon scurrying about. "Just a raccoon," he whispered.

UW Campus

Sam approached her dorm on foot. She saw the light above the outside door had burned out. She heard someone walking behind her, and glanced over her shoulder to see a man's silhouette. She quickened her pace, but the man gained on her. She gulped air, trying to move quickly without looking panicked.

At this time of night, the outside door of the dorm would be locked. She pulled the wad of keys from her pocket, trying to find the right one. In the darkness all the keys looked similar.

She found the correct one as she reached the building. She heard the man, not more than twenty-five feet behind her. She fumbled with the lock for an instant, then jerked the door open. She squeezed inside and tried to pull the door shut, but the cylinder mounted at the top of the door resisted her tug.

The man reached the outside of the glass door, grabbed the handle, and pulled back. Sam shrieked and ran toward the stairs.

"Wait! Police!"

Sam looked over her shoulder as she continued to run. Her pursuer wore a uniform. She stopped, but with her body tensed and ready to resume flight.

"I'm sorry, miss. I didn't mean to scare you. Are you Samantha Trzebiatowski?"

"Why do you want to know?"

"You may be in danger. Come with me to the police station and I'll explain."

Cedar Park

Back in the van, Burrell grew frustrated. "Damn it!" he swore. "Why aren't they showing up? Something's wrong. Really wrong." He spoke to the tactical leader. "What the hell's going on out there? Aren't you guys seeing anything?"

"Negative. There isn't a single living thing in this park other than Kent and some rodents."

Burrell thought for a moment. "Oh, shit! Has anyone swept through that apartment just over the hill?"

"Negative. There's a large open area between the apartments and the park, and the windows of the buildings are all below the crest of the hill. If someone approached from there, we'd see them in plenty of time."

"What about the roof?"

"There's a city cop in an unmarked car on the other side."

"He's sitting two blocks down. He won't be able to see the roof! Can you see the complex from where you're at?"

"Negative. I don't have a very good view. Number Two, do you read?"

"Number Two here. I'm looking."

Kent couldn't hear any of this conversation, and didn't know why Burrell had been silent. Could communications have been cut? He was terrified. He breathed heavily, and despite the cold night, sweat ran down his sides.

"I think I see someone on the roof," Number Two reported. "It looked like a head was briefly visible over the peak."

"Number Two," the tactical leader directed, "reposition yourself if necessary to get a clear view. Don't take your eyes off that roof."

"I see him again," Number Two reported. "He appears to have a gun."

"Kent, get down!" Burrell ordered over the radio.

Kent dropped off the bench and flattened himself to the ground.

"Fire!" the tactical leader commanded.

Number Two struggled for a clear view of the man on the roof because of tree branches swaying in the heavy breeze.

Yuri crouched on the roof with a .30-.30 semi-automatic rifle equipped with a silencer. Most of his body stayed hidden below the back side of the roof, with only his head, shoulders and arms over the peak. He had Kent in his ambient light scope, and had been ready to shoot when Kent flung himself off the park bench. "Damn!" Yuri whispered. He realized someone must have spotted him. He had to finish his job, though—there might not be a second chance. He aimed at Kent again. He would have to fire through the wooden back of the park bench to reach Kent on the ground. He would shoot several rounds to be sure. He had the illuminated cross hairs trained on the correct spot. His right index finger tightened on the sensitive trigger.

A round of ammo quietly slipped through the night air. Yuri dropped the gun, and slumped over the peak of the roof, his forehead blown away by the sharpshooter on the ground. His gun slid down the rough shingles and caught on the rain gutter.

Sergey, who waited in the Mustang below, realized what had happened and drove off. The tires squealed as he turned sharply out of the parking lot, the car roaring down the street.

"After him!" Burrell ordered the van driver, who started the engine and popped it in drive. He floored the pedal, and Burrell flew back in the van, hitting the steel doors. He regained his balance and stepped over to the electronic equipment. "Get Kent out of there right away," he instructed the tactical leader. Then he switched to the regular police frequency and contacted dispatch. "This is Agent Burrell. We're in pursuit of a black Mustang heading westbound on Cedar Street near the park. Requesting backup."

"Acknowledged," dispatch replied.

The van continued to follow the Mustang, trailing by several blocks. The Mustang turned several times, but traffic remained light, and the driver of the van had a good view every time the Mustang changed direction. Finally, the Mustang ducked into an alley just short of an intersection on the other side of a parked delivery truck. The FBI driver thought Sergey had turned at the intersection, so he shot past the alley.

Sergey went through the alley and headed back toward the park.

An approaching FBI car spotted the black Mustang and swerved in front of it to cut it off. Sergey stopped short of the other car, whipped it in reverse, and shot the other direction.

The van crossed the street in front of Sergey. The Russian stomped on the brake pedal, cranked the wheel, and slid sideways before coming to an abrupt stop. He bailed out of the car and ran through a narrow gap between two buildings.

On the other side, a city police car approached from two blocks away, and Sergey scanned his surroundings for an escape route. Running through alleys in an unfamiliar city swarming with cops would certainly get him caught, he realized.

The street had been torn up thirty feet away, and a manhole cover had been left off in the barricaded area. Sergey ran to the construction zone, picked up a barricade, and smashed it on the street three times to dislodge a blinking orange light. The legs broke off, but both lights clung to the top board, the pulse of one stopping. He picked up the board with lights attached and slipped down the manhole.

Burrell emerged from the alley just in time to see the *mafiya* hit man crawl under the street. He ran to the barricaded area, and could hear the slosh of Sergey's footsteps echoing through the wet subterranean passage. The agent turned his head to see a city police car pull up. Two young cops jumped out.

"CIA," Burrell said, flashing his ID. "Gimme your Mag Lite."

One officer drew a flashlight from his belt and handed it to Burrell, who cautiously peered into the hole. He set the flashlight down, pulled his suit coat off and dangled it in the hole with the light shining on it. No one fired at his coat.

"Have someone guard every manhole cover for miles," Burrell ordered as he put his coat on and started into the hole with the light off. "How big is the storm sewer anyway?"

"You're going in there?" one officer asked.

"I don't see anybody else volunteering," he said, as the blacktop swallowed his legs.

"You're lucky," the other officer answered. "The storm sewers in this part of town are big enough to walk through, but you might have to hunch over a bit. In most parts of Madison, they're only about a foot in diameter."

The agent disappeared into the bowels of the city and remained stooped to avoid hitting his head. He strained to hear over his pounding heart and heavy breathing, as his eyes started to adjust to the darkness. The faint sound of footsteps reverberated through the tunnel, making it difficult to determine the direction from which it originated. The tinkling of a small stream of water competed with the noise Sergey made.

After a moment looking back and forth down the tunnel, Burrell noticed a weak flash of orange light bouncing off the wall perhaps a couple blocks away. Sergey must have turned a corner, he thought. He turned the light on and shined it both directions to make sure Sergey wasn't in sight. Seeing no one and knowing his path was clear, he turned off the light and started to run, straddling the stream of water in the middle to minimize the noise.

Dank air and claustrophobic thoughts started to cloud his mind as he ran awkwardly, hands out and feet far apart, through the confining darkness. He stopped after a moment to listen again, and hearing nothing, resumed pursuit.

Running farther, he stopped as the clang from a manhole cover dropping echoed around him. Burrell wasn't sure if the Russian had escaped and replaced the lid to hide his point of escape or if he'd failed to get the lid up far enough and dropped it back in place while remaining in the tunnel.

The orange flashing light reappeared after being absent for a minute. Burrell slowed, walking as quietly as he could in leather-soled wingtips on the debris-strewn path. The CIA operative tensed his hand on his gun. He didn't dare turn on the flashlight, lest he become an easy target.

The orange strobe was bright enough now to define the edges of an intersecting passage. He flattened himself to one wall as he inched forward. The sound of trickling water rippled through the silence.

The tunnel boomed with a staccato rhythm and Burrell jumped. Then he realized a truck had run over a manhole cover. He resumed his movement forward until he reached the intersecting sewer. He stood, heart pounding, light flashing. He waited until he felt synchronized with the light, and when the light extinguished, he swung his gun around the corner just as the lamp flashed back on.

The Russian stood to the side, body partly concealed around another corner where the tunnel widened into a small room. Burrell and Sergey fired simultaneously, barrels spitting fire with a deafening roar as darkness enveloped them for another instant. Burrell couldn't tell if he hit his target, but Sergey's bullet missed its mark and ricocheted off the walls.

The CIA man jumped back to the safety offered by the corner. Breathing harder, with his ears ringing loudly, he struggled to determine his next move.

Sergey would be having just as difficult time hearing after that blast, Burrell realized. He synchronized himself to the pulsing light again and crouched, ready to spring. As the bulb switched off, he leapt across the entrance of the intersecting tunnel.

From his new vantage point, he could see the bulb without exposing himself to Sergey. He inched his head over to the side along with his gun. When the light flashed on again, he fired, extinguishing the strobe permanently.

He felt like his ears were going to bleed from the repeated cracks of confined thunder, and he covered his ears with a hand and a forearm. After a moment, he got down on his hands and knees. Inhaling deeply to catch his breath after minutes of shallow breathing to remain silent, the rotten odor from the tunnel floor sickened him. With the gun in one hand and flashlight in the other, he crawled to stay below possible gunfire, sharp pebbles cutting into his skin.

He could hear nothing of his own movements over the persistent ringing, and he hoped Sergey would be similarly handicapped. It was difficult to gauge the distance he covered. After what seemed like two or three minutes, he stopped. There was no opportunity for error or missed shots. Once he switched on the light, he would be completely vulnerable.

Burrell played out his next move in his head, sweating profusely despite the frigid tunnel. Then he gulped in air and threw himself onto his back as he switched the flashlight on. Sergey was right above him, gun pointed out rather than down. Burrell tensed and unloaded three rounds into the Russian's belly.

Sergey fell on him, gushing blood and bile. The agent, not sure if Sergey had died, violently threw him off as he jumped to his feet. Sergey continued to clutch his gun, and Burrell stepped on it and kicked the gun away with a flick of his heel. Sergey twitched, his neck twisted grotesquely with the one visible eye unmoving.

Burrell stepped over to the Russian's gun, popped the clip, and ejected the shell from the chamber. He set the gun down and slipped the clip and loose round into his coat pocket. He placed two fingers on the side of the man's trachea, and detecting no pulse, walked below the manhole cover.

He holstered his pistol and climbed the ladder, shining the light down every couple seconds to make sure the Russian wasn't moving, despite knowing his adversary had died. A wave of claustrophobia swept over him. He thrust a shoulder and his opposite hand at the heavy cover, sliding it to the side. He jumped out onto the street.

Burrell cut through the darkness below with the light, and shuddered when he didn't see the *mafiya* figure. He moved the light and his head, and felt relieved when the man's feet came into view. He dusted himself and tried to regain his composure as the CIA van swung into view.

CHAPTER FORTY-ONE

Moscow

FSB Agent Kalugin's shift had just ended, and on his way home he decided to stop for coffee. He entered a little restaurant in a gray, concrete building, slumped onto a chair, letting his heavy eyelids drop at the same time. A moment later he opened his eyes and let his gaze drift from face to face. In a corner across the room, the profile of a man caught his attention. Kalugin squinted to be sure, then eased out of his chair and located a phone. Reaching his immediate superior on the line, he whispered, "I thought we had Kardirov covered?"

"We do. Why?"

"Because I stopped for coffee on my way home, and now I'm looking at him."

"That can't be—not five minutes ago I got a report of visual confirmation that he was home in his apartment."

"Somebody better double-check. The guy's right here—birthmark and everything."

"What's he doing?"

"Talking to a tall guy with glasses. I haven't been able to hear anything they're saying."

"Well, stay on 'em. I'll have someone else there in three minutes."

Kalugin ordered coffee and sipped it while discretely watching the two men. He wanted to look straight at them to see if he could read their lips, but figured he'd be noticed. He could hear the inflections of their voices. Kardirov's companion sounded worried, talking in hurried whispers. One word was audible: "Iranians."

Kalugin looked at his watch and then out the glass door. Still no sign of backup.

Kirill Kardirov rose from his table, and the tall man jumped to his feet, catching the edge of the table with his leg. The jolt sloshed water out of their two glasses. Kardirov frowned and walked outside, turning left. The tall man stayed back for a moment, mopping up some of the water with a napkin while looking about. When he exited the building, he walked to the right. Kalugin threw some money on the table, and counted out the time: one second ... two seconds ... three seconds ... this seemed like an eternity when he couldn't see what they were doing or where they were going ... four seconds ... five seconds. He could not risk having them know he trailed them.

He strolled outside and swept the surroundings with his eyes. Kardirov had just climbed into the backseat of a car—not his usual Mercedes.

Kalugin panicked for a moment, thinking he would lose Kardirov, but then spotted two agents in a car across the street. He gave a slight nod, then walked to the right to follow the tall man.

As the two agents in the car shadowed Kardirov's vehicle, they saw him put his cell phone to his ear.

"Damn!" the driver of the FSB car said. "We got all this eavesdropping equipment, but I know it's scrambled."

"I'm recording it anyway," replied the other agent. "Maybe ten years from now we can unscramble it and figure out what he said."

Eight days later

The briefing room of the Moscow Organized Crime Combat Department (GUVD) bristled with tension and anticipation as the elite group of officers received their instructions for crushing Volkov's organization in Moscow. Most listened in disbelief as they learned the U.S. government had decoded Kirill Kardirov's phone conversations in a matter of days. They did not know about Kent's decryption technology and the adaptation of that technology to coded voice transmissions.

"With the information provided by the Americans, the arrest of Nikolai Volkov, and the capture of several participants in the nuclear train robbery, we're ready to attack Volkov's operation," said the GUVD leader. "Kardirov is keeping things running, and capturing him, alive if possible, is our highest priority. We've all studied their facilities and weaknesses as part of our ongoing surveillance, so I expect you to be able to shut 'em down later today."

"Are we going to call in the MVD militia to assist?" one officer asked, referring to the regular police force under the control of the Ministry of the Interior.

"No. We can't risk forewarning Kardirov, so we're keeping this quiet. I'm sure the MVD will feel left out, but we can't risk a leak, particularly with the sensitive national security issues involved."

The GUVD spent the day planning a coordinated assault on numerous facilities, which would commence at 3:00 a.m. when Volkov's security would be weakest and the waxing crescent moon would be well below the horizon, providing the cover of darkness. The men retired early to bunk beds, with no one allowed to leave headquarters or contact the outside, for fear the *mafiya* had penetrated the GUVD.

At 1:45 a.m., the organized crime combat forces, having rested fitfully, loaded into three primary trucks, one bound for Kirill Kardirov's residence, one for Volkov's headquarters, and one for a trucking company controlled by Volkov. Several cars and vans drove to smaller offices connected with the "wolf" of organized crime. By 2:30, all forces were deployed near their targets.

The building thought to be Volkov's headquarters posed the greatest challenge for the GUVD. A chain-link fence with a heavy steel gate surrounded a wide open area in which semi's could load and unload from the mammoth concrete and glass block building at the center. Cement barriers eliminated the possibility of ramming the fence with a truck. Twelve men patrolled the grounds, four in front (the southern side), four in back and two on each side, with automatic rifles hanging from shoulder straps.

Officers established control of neighboring buildings, and six snipers took positions on the roofs.

At 2:40, a blaze erupted at a warehouse two blocks north of Volkov's facility, a building long used for surveillance of the criminal inhabitants of the area. Within fifteen minutes, sirens wailed as fire trucks and ambulances rushed to the fire. A petroleum storage tank exploded, drawing the guards' attention. Two remained near the entrance while the rest moved to the back.

GUVD snipers fired at the isolated guards in the front, dropping them instantly. A pickup truck raced to the gate and parked sideways. Two men jumped out of the back, one with a cutting torch connected by heavy rubber hoses to acetylene and oxygen tanks in the truck, the other held a sledgehammer for additional "persuasion."

The man with the torch opened the gas valves as soon as his feet hit the pavement, and lit it before he made it to the gate. Kneeling, he adjusted the flame to even out the four blue cones shooting from the nozzle. The locking bar on the gate, although thick, couldn't withstand the torch. The officer with the sledge wrenched the gate open as the flame finished its work. They jumped into the box of the truck as it pulled away from the gate and sped down the road.

No sooner had the pickup cleared the gate than a delivery truck smashed into the compound. It swung alongside the building at a rapid pace, but eased to a stop. Twenty men flowed out the back, eighteen dressed in black with Kevlar armor, the remaining two wore clothes similar to the guards. The two dragged the bodies of the guards and deposited them in the truck. One then ran to the gate and shut it, using a weak cord to temporarily hold it.

The eighteen GUVD officers fanned out, taking positions by walk-in doors, loading ramps, and corners of the building. Six of them, having secured two ropes to the roof, began to scale the 30-foot high walls.

Once the men on the roof confirmed their positions by radio, the tactical leader gave the order to strike. Silenced shots rained down in three-round bursts on the guards staring at the nearby fire. One member of the building security team turned and pointed his automatic at the roof, but had no time to pinpoint his target before being cut to pieces by steel-jacketed bullets.

The perimeter secure, two officers in front slapped sheets of explosive material onto the walk-in doors, and whirled to the side as they detonated the charges. The doors ripped off their hinges and slammed to the floor. A second man at each door pointed the muzzle of his submachine gun into the opening and fired a flash/bang grenade from a barrel-mounted launcher. Blinding flashes of light accompanied by a series of explosions stunned several men inside.

The GUVD forces poured in the doors and leveled their guns at armed thugs. An exchange of gunfire erupted. Volkov's men quickly fell.

The assault team spotted what appeared to be a heavily-fortified second-story office area. The occupants would now know of the attack and would be difficult to root out. As the team ran toward the office area, shots sputtered across the warehouse floor, and two officers dropped in pools of blood. The gunman met the same fate a few seconds later.

The office door opened an instant, and a fragmentation grenade tumbled down the steps. The GUVD men dove for cover, but shrapnel caught three of them, killing one and severely injuring the other two.

The mafiosi in the office, after igniting documents and several computers with gasoline, escaped through a narrow passageway and exited at the rear of the building. The snipers on the roof mowed them down as they ran toward a van.

Firefighters, rushing from two blocks away, quickly extinguished the blaze in Volkov's office, but not before most records burned. With the building secured, the warehouse tactical leader radioed his counterparts. Kardirov had been captured, sustaining a non-fatal bullet wound to the shoulder, and one GUVD officer lost his life before reaching Kardirov. Kardirov's only break from prison would be his short stay in the hospital for treatment of his shoulder.

Timothy S. Jacobson

EPILOGUE

Madison

The day after the incident in Cedar Park, Federal agents relocated Daltons. John and Kent received only several hours to pack their most important items, and then flew to Phoenix accompanied by FBI agents. The rest of their belongings followed a short time later. New identities were assigned to John and Kent, and John took a job in a lab.

On a Saturday three weeks after arriving in Phoenix, Kent lay alone in his new bedroom, the eggshell-painted walls bare. John had left for the day, and Kent felt crushed by loneliness and the knowledge he had completely disrupted his life and that of his father. He felt so alien, suddenly uprooted from the city where he had spent his whole life. He missed having a yard deep with snow now that it was winter. "Gene is probably in the middle of a snowball fight with some other kid," Kent thought. Madison had been hit by a winter storm the night before according to the Weather Channel.

He rolled onto his side and looked down at a picture frame, filled only with a sheet of glass, leaning against the base of the wall and reflecting back a faint image of his face. He studied his eyes for a moment and thought back to the dream he had the night he and Gene blew up the dumpster, the dream where someone lurked in the background as the police caught him. It was no longer a mystery who had caused his undoing.

Kent's thoughts turned to Sam. He both despised her and missed her. The memory of the fresh scent of her hair from the time he lay on the bed next to her suddenly filled his head.

He walked across his bedroom to an unpacked box, rummaged a moment, and pulled out a spiral bound notebook. He went to his desk, fished a pen out of the drawer, sat down and began to write:

Dear Sam,

I was happy when I heard that the police located you and you were okay. I bet that whole incident had you shaken up a bit.

I assume you heard about my run-in with the Russian *mafiya*. I'm very sorry you got brought into this. I've caused a lot of pain for a lot of people—you and your family, Gene and his family, and my dad and me. I'm under the federal witness protection program, and they've relocated us. I'll be testifying in court if Volkov goes to trial.

I assume you've also heard from the UW administration what I did to your transcript. I sent a couple nasty e-mails from your account too. I'm sorry. I did it because I checked your e-mail account to make sure it was working, and saw the note you wrote to Chris. Needless to say, I was hurt by what you wrote. You didn't have to pretend to like me just to get me to help with your homework. I shouldn't have done what I did anyway. I guess I knew you were using me, but I didn't want to believe it. Maybe I was using you too.

Kent looked at the page for a long time, struggling to find words to express his feelings, as memories churned in his brain. He signed the letter, ripped the page from the notebook, and stuffed it in an envelope. For mail using his real identity, he had to route it through U.S. Marshals to avoid a postmark disclosing his location. He set the envelope on his desk.

Then he got up, slowly walked downstairs, and went outside. A strong breeze tossed his hair back. Featureless clouds stretched across the expanse of sky. As he sat on the front steps, a cool drop struck his cheek. He pulled his knees against his chest and wrapped his arms around his legs. He watched cars driving by and people scurrying to get out of the light rain. These were people, Kent thought, who had normal identities, people who didn't worry about the *mafiya* pursuing them.

Madison
April

Attorney Michael Maurer buried his fingers under his hair and squeezed his temples with the palms of his hands as he closed his eyes. He sighed and turned his back to the little gray table behind which Volkov sat. "I give up," Maurer said at last.

"You give up? I don't know why I've paid you so much fucking money," Volkov shouted. Then he took a drag from his smoldering cigarette and lowered his voice. "I could have bought off the judge with all I've paid you. I mean, what the hell are you doing? You filed a whole bunch of pretrial motions that didn't get me anywhere, and I've been sitting in this damn jail for months."

Maurer turned to face his client. "Nick, you gotta work with me here. I've been telling you over and over that unless you give some high-level people up, the U.S. attorney is going to take this to trial." Maurer leaned forward and set his palms down on the edge of the table. "They've got plenty to seek the death penalty, and even in liberal Madison, they're not going to have much of a problem frying a *mafiya* figure involved in stealing plutonium and trying to run over a kid with a car. Cutting a deal isn't likely to spare you from life in prison, but it should save you from execution."

Volkov glared at Maurer, then looked down at the table. A moment later, he lifted his eyes. "I think I have something your government will like. I know there are Americans in Colombia working covertly and getting their asses whipped while trying to fight the drug trade. There are Russians down there working with the Colombians, and that's why the Americans are doing so poorly." Volkov inhaled deeply on his Marlboro. "I wouldn't mind seeing one particular Russian go down. His name is Leonard Korshakov. I can provide detailed evidence linking him to the drug trade both in the U.S. and in Colombia."

Kent and Gene were eventually charged with several counts of illegal computer activities. Each provided a statement to assist in prosecuting Volkov, and entered a guilty plea in exchange for dismissal of most charges and arguments for leniency by the prosecutor.

At the appointed day for Kent's sentencing, he and his dad took a car to the federal courthouse, a modern, dark blue building with rounded corners. They managed to snag a parking space on the street right out front.

The Daltons entered, and were greeted by three people providing building security. The Daltons had to empty metal objects from their pockets, and Kent made the mistake of carrying a pocket knife. It got deposited in a manila envelope for retrieval upon leaving the building. Then they passed through metal detectors and took an elevator to the second floor.

They met Kent's defense attorney fifteen minutes before his scheduled court appearance to review what would happen. The three of them walked into the courtroom.

Even though this wasn't Kent's first visit to the courthouse, the look of the courtroom surprised him. The walls and judge's bench echoed the blue contours of the building's exterior. Numerous TV monitors, used for displaying exhibits, had been placed around the room. At first Kent noticed only two people present in the room, apparently an attorney and his client waiting for sentencing in another matter. As he turned to the right, he spotted a U.S. Marshal standing by a side door.

Kent's lawyer motioned for him and his father to follow as he walked toward the front of the room. John sat just behind the low wall separating counsel tables from the bench seating in the rear, while Kent went through the swinging gate and sat at the defense table with his lawyer. A moment later the prosecutor, a middle-aged woman, entered the courtroom, greeted Kent's attorney, sat down, and shuffled some papers.

Five tense minutes passed before the judge, also a woman, entered the room, dressed in a black robe, along with her clerk and court reporter. The U.S. Marshal commanded all to rise.

The judge called Kent's case, United States versus Kent Dalton, then noted the appearances of the parties for the record. The judge covered the procedural status of the case and asked for comments from the attorneys.

After Kent's attorney and the prosecutor had spoken about the nature of the offenses and the mitigating factors to be considered, the judge looked straight into Kent's eyes. "Do you care to make a statement, Mr. Dalton?" she asked sternly.

"I, I just want to say I'm sorry for all the trouble I've caused, and I'm not going to do anything like this again."

"Mr. Dalton, I take my job very seriously. I feel a certain sense of personal responsibility for what happens to you and people like you after I hand down the sentence, particularly in a case where I believe the defendant has a good shot at cleaning up his or her act and accomplishing something positive for society. I sit here with mixed feelings. I understand you risked your life to assist in apprehending vicious members of the Russian *mafiya*. Also, apparently through the information and technology you provided to authorities, several members of the *mafiya* were caught in Russia and millions of dollars in stolen assets and cash seized. For that, you live the rest of your life in danger."

The judge adjusted her glasses and continued, "On the other hand, your predicament is of your own doing. If you had not engaged in criminal conduct, you would not have encountered the *mafiya*. And while your computer activities may have seemed innocuous at the time, it is clear you interfered with the work of countless individuals. I don't know how you justified your criminal activities to yourself, or whether you bothered to justify them at all, but your actions were harmful. There is a reason for the laws we have. When people like you ignore the rules, the long-term cost to society is enormous. I hope you've learned many valuable lessons from this, and I hope I never have to see you here after today.

"I've been struggling with how to sentence you. I need to fashion a punishment that protects society while at the same time helping to ensure you will be a law-abiding, productive citizen. Given the mitigating factors here, I think jail time is inappropriate. I am going to sentence you to two years of probation. As terms of that probation, I have seriously considered prohibiting you from the use of computers, but I'm not going to do that. I've been informed that one of your programming projects has the potential to help thousands of individuals who suffer from the loss of limbs, and from paralysis. You need to learn to focus your talent on legal means of achieving your goals and God willing, you will. Instead of keeping you from computers, I am going to impose 250 hours of community service which can be fulfilled by assisting charitable organizations with their computing needs.

You will be fined $7,500, and the money seized from your bank account will be used to satisfy that fine. I'm also going to impose restitution for any of the victims of your worm program who care to file a claim. If you successfully complete your probation, I'll order expungement of this conviction from your record, particularly since this is your first offense."

The judge took her eyes off of Kent and looked at the prosecutor. "Is there anything further?"

"No, your Honor."

The judge then stood, and everyone snapped to their feet as she exited to her chambers. Kent turned to his father. John, his brow furrowed with concern, mustered a weak smile to reassure his son. Kent turned back to face his lawyer who shook his hand.

"Good luck, Kent," the lawyer said with a wink.

Kent walked over to his dad, looked down pensively, and then returned his gaze to his father's face. "I'm sorry, Dad."

John attempted another smile. "Let's go home." He put his arm around Kent's shoulders as they walked out of the courtroom together.

ABOUT THE AUTHOR

Timothy S. Jacobson is an attorney who has served as president of a law firm, chief techie geek of a dot-com business, executive producer of documentaries, historical interpreter and blacksmith for a living history museum, executive of a privately-held energy company, and executive director of a nonprofit conservancy. *Law & Politics* and *Milwaukee Magazine* named him a "Super Lawyer" in 2005. He is admitted to practice before the United States Supreme Court. *USA Today* said, "If … Jacobson['s firm] isn't careful, it may wind up giving lawyers a good name." *Saint Paul Pioneer Press* called his firm "one of the most Internet-savvy law firms in existence." The conservancy he runs received recognition as "Land Trust of the Year" and "Friend of Conservation – Outstanding Organization." *La Crosse Tribune* proclaimed Jacobson "King of the Hills" in a front-page article. He has served on the board of directors for multiple for-profit companies and nonprofit organizations, and he is a frequent public speaker.

He is an instrument-rated airplane pilot, as well as being a mission pilot and squadron legal officer with the rank of major in the Civil Air Patrol, the official auxiliary of the U.S. Air Force. In addition, Jacobson has a black belt in karate and an advanced scuba diving certification. He enjoys playing guitar and writing songs, hiking, skiing, rock climbing, kayaking, world travel and study of languages, blacksmithing, filmmaking, writing, skydiving, calligraphy, drawing, reading, taxidermy, juggling and computer programming.